A Beautiful Prison

by
Jenika Snow

Copyright © 2014 Jenika Snow
   Published by Jenika Snow
   www.JenikaSnow.com
   Jenika_Snow@yahoo.com
   Digital Edition
   First E-book Publication: March 2014
   Smashwords Edition
   Cover design by Sloan Winters
   Edited by Editing by Rebecca

   WARNING: This is a Dark Erotic story. This is not a traditional love story. This book is fiction and contains material readers may find offensive. There is very disturbing content, graphic sex, violence, and strong language, but does end with a HEA.

Ruby Jacobson wanted a new life, but it seems fate gives her a twisted version of it. Taken from her bed, and sold like an object, Ruby believes death is a far better outcome then what fate has in store for her. Or so she thought.

Gavin Darris has always desired the darker pleasures in life. Normally not one to purchase his playthings, he needs a woman who will bend to his will, and derive pleasure from it, too. He sees Ruby, one of the many women for sale, and he wants her as he's never wanted anything else before. She has a fire in her eyes and a determination not to yield. She looks like a fighter and is exactly what he is looking for. Making her submit will be almost as pleasurable as finally sating the darkness inside of him.

He is ruthless in what he wants, and what he wants is Ruby.

The dark desires Ruby has felt inside of her are about to be tempted in the most horrifying of ways. She should hate Gavin and fear everything he represents, but she can't deny that her body aches for his touch. He tells her she is his; that he owns every part of her, and everything inside of her knows that is the truth.

Faced with the ultimate decision, Ruby must choose to escape and gain her freedom, or stay with Gavin, the monster whose delicious punishment makes her yearn for more.

Both are frightening.

Preface

She was his.

Irrevocably. Undeniably.

He knew this as soon as he saw her bound on the stage. He needed to possess her, own her, and make sure she knew that he was the one that held all the power. She was his property now, whether she accepted that or not. She would soon come to realize that there was no escape.

He had bought her, picked her from all the other women that had been taken and sold like nothing more than inanimate objects. However, she wasn't just an object. She was *his* to do with as he pleased.

She looked at him with fear, but she hadn't felt real fear yet. He was a monster, the kind that she had probably dreamt about as a child, prayed she would never meet, and one that now owned her.

She would run, there was no doubt about that, but what she would soon realize was he wanted her to. He reveled in the chase, and when he caught her, he'd make her pay with her body until she gave him every part of herself.

He was a sadist, and with each passing day, she would realize that she was his perfect masochist.

Chapter One

It was sweet, beautiful pain that filled her mind, washed through her, and had her needy for more. She wanted to stay here forever, in this dream that seemed to haunt her nightly. However, she couldn't really say it haunted her, not when she prayed for the sweet release it brought her every night before she closed her eyes. Disgust and shame filled her each morning when she reflected on those dreams. For pain *with* pleasure wasn't "normal," right? It made no difference because it was only in her dreams that she would allow these dark desires to control her. She enjoyed the idea of marks on her flesh, a hand on her throat, slowly tightening until darkness threatened to take her away. Only in her dreams could she ever allow herself that moment of depravity.

An outraged scream and the sound of something shattering had Ruby slowly opening her eyes. She blinked a few times, but otherwise stayed in the bed, her comforter that smelled faintly of mold pulled up to her chin, and stared at the ceiling. It was off-white, but riddled with brown stains. Her mother yelled something nasty and ugly, presumably at her boyfriend. Ruby thought his name was Buck, or maybe it was Chuck. She didn't really know or care since there seemed to be a new one every week. With her graduation already past, it was finally time for her to leave. She had been thinking about this moment for years and time had finally come.

Ruby was going to leave this shitty city behind her, forget about the ugliness that surrounded her every single day, and start over. She didn't even have a set plan, but she didn't need one because she just didn't care. The idea of spending one more moment surrounded by the failings of her upbringing was enough to push her out the door. She'd work things out when she got to Fort Hampton. Maybe she would fail and feel just as misplaced as she did right now, but she wouldn't know unless she tried. If she stayed here another moment longer, she knew she wouldn't survive.

Her mind felt like it was deteriorating with every harsh comment that left her mother's mouth and with every inhalation of this smog-filled air. With a trailer to call home, a reputation as "trash" all through high school, and no friends, Ruby was used to feeling as if she didn't belong. Yes, she isolated herself, but she found that being alone was a much better existence. The waste that surrounded her, the feelings of emptiness, and no self-worth was something Ruby knew, but not something she wanted. There was a big world out there, one that she could explore and hopefully, start to feel like she was finally living.

She pushed up on the bed and the comforter fell away from her body. She hadn't fallen asleep until well after midnight, courtesy of her mother and the boyfriend of the week having sex in the next room. The paper-thin walls did nothing to block out the sound of a banging headboard and the vile things the two said to each other. Scrubbing her hands over her face, she dropped them and exhaled. She reached over and grabbed her cell. Flipping it open, she stared at the lit screen. It was only five-thirty in the morning and already the yelling had started. Tossing the cheap phone back on her scarred bedside table, she decided she'd rather be sitting at the bus stop than stay here one more minute. It was only a matter of time before her mother took out her anger on Ruby.

After she had her jeans on, she grabbed a T-shirt and slipped it over her head. Getting on her knees and reaching under her bed, she felt for the straps of her backpack and wrapped her fingers around it. Once she pulled it out, she reached inside for her ratty hoodie. It was ugly as hell, but well loved. She grabbed the one-way ticket to Fort Hampton and moved her fingers over it. It was a fourteen-hour bus ride, and she had no idea what she would do once she got there, but anything was better than this. She tucked the ticket in the bag next to her money. Once she had her hoodie and her shoes on, she sat back on her bed. It was sad that everything she owned fit into this bag. Clothes, the thousand dollars she had saved from working at the fast food place down the street, and a few personal items were all inside the confines of the canvas. Although she had no definitive plans once she got to Fort Hampton, she had researched some cheap places she could stay. She had restaurant experience, well, fast food experience, but she was hoping to find something of that nature to do as soon as she got there. The thousand dollars she had wouldn't last her very long.

Standing and slinging her bag over her shoulders, she moved toward her door and waited a moment to see if there would be any more yelling. She pulled it open as silently as she could and listened again. Should she have felt guilt over the fact she planned to leave without telling the woman that had given birth to her? Maybe she would if that woman had actually acted like a mother in the first place.

The lights were on, and she stepped out of her room shutting the door quietly behind her. If her mom was fighting with Buck/Chuck, she would already be in a foul mood. The sound of the TV was low, but she didn't let that distract her. Ruby kept her eyes averted to the ground and made her way toward the front door.

"And where the hell do you think you're going?" On instinct, Ruby stopped and looked over at Missy Jacobson, her mother and the woman that treated her like she shit on the bottom of her shoe. She sat at the cracked, faded yellow Formica kitchen table, littered with cigarette burns. A bottle of whiskey in front of her, the glass beside it was nearly empty. The bags under her mom's eyes were dark, and it was clear she hadn't gone to bed yet. Missy lifted the cigarette she held to her mouth and inhaled deeply. She pulled it away and flicked the ash into the small aluminum tray beside the liquor bottle. "You gonna answer me or stand there like a fucking idiot?" she said at the same time she exhaled all that smoke.

Ruby tightened her hold on one strap of her bag. "I have work early today." Telling her mom that she was leaving for good would only cause a fight, especially since Ruby had been giving part of her paycheck to Missy since she started working. With this being her only home, it was either help keep this piece of shit trailer afloat or have her mom kick her out. Finishing school had been a priority for Ruby, so she sucked it up and told herself that as soon as she had her diploma she would be out of there. Today was that day, and Missy Jacobson wasn't going to ruin it.

"Is that right?" Missy took another puff from her cigarette and exhaled. "Then why you need that backpack? Flipping burgers and filling up Styrofoam cups doesn't require a lot of books."

"I have to go."

"I need money for rent."

Ruby stopped and looked over at her mom. "I just gave you some last week."

Missy shrugged. "What can I say? Keeping your big ass in this house costs money. There's electricity, water, rent. A lot of shit."

"I don't have any more." Missy narrowed her eyes.

"Girl, I put up with your ass prancing around here in your damn underwear, trying to tempt my men. You're fucking lucky I let you even live here. You're more damn trouble than you're worth." Ruby wasn't about to argue over the fact she sure as hell didn't prance around anywhere in just her underwear. In fact, she rarely came out of her room when she was home, not after one of her mother's boyfriends tried to touch her. Missy poured herself another shot and tipped the glass back to her lips. Her eyes were glossy and red-rimmed, and Ruby knew she was drunk, probably had been since yesterday. "I should have aborted your ass when I found out I was pregnant." Bile rose in Ruby's stomach. Even though nothing her mom said was sweet and loving, and was always vile in nature, it still hurt like hell.

"I'll bring you some money after work."

Missy leaned back in the seat. "You better or you can kiss your room goodbye."

Ruby stared at her mom for another second. "Bye."

Missy didn't even respond, just stared straight ahead, and smoked. Ruby felt no sadness in leaving. In fact, there was a very deep comfort in the knowledge that this was the last time she would step foot in this shithole. Anything was better than this, including sleeping under a bridge, which might be a possibility once she reached Fort Hampton.

Ruby wrapped her arms around her middle when a gust of wind whipped by her. The sound of the approaching bus and her cramping stomach had woken her from a somewhat restless sleep. She had been at the bus station all day, sleeping off and on as best she could with the noise all around her. She had only had a granola bar and a bottle of water since she left the trailer. She could have eaten something a bit more substantial, but she wanted to save every penny for Fort Hampton.

Straightening as the bus pulled to a stop, she noticed that several people lined up to get on the Greyhound. The smell of burning rubber from the bus braking and the exhaust filling the air around her had Ruby covering her mouth and nose with her hoodie. The door on the bus slid open and people inside started piling out. When the last person stepped off the bus, it was a few minutes before anyone could get on as the attendants cleaned it. Ruby glanced at the people waiting to load. There were a few families with children in tow, some college-aged kids, and the occasional elderly person. She glanced along the row of people once more and her gaze stopped at one of the several benches that lined the side of the bus station. A man in a long black trench coat held a newspaper in his lap, his attention on her.

He didn't look very old, maybe in his early twenties, with brown hair slicked back from his face, and eyes that looked black and bottomless. There was a clear darkness inside of him, and even though they were several feet apart, Ruby felt a very uncomfortable sensation move along the length of her spine. What she should have done was look away, but there was an invisible force keeping their gazes locked. She didn't know him, had never seen him before, but he made her feel like he could see into her soul, and knew every secret she held.

She quickly glanced away, tightened her hold on the backpack in her lap, and felt very uneasy all of a sudden. She still felt his stare boring into her, so she stood, needing to get on the bus and put some distance between them. Why did she have this sudden sense of wariness? Maybe her situation had her on edge. The knowledge that she didn't know what her life would be like. That rationalization had her easing slightly because it seemed logical enough.

Ruby took her place in line and waited as everyone loaded onto the bus. Maybe she shouldn't have, but she found herself glancing at where the young man had been sitting. A breath left her, one that she hadn't realized she had been holding, when she saw he was no longer sitting there. Yes, she was overreacting, seeing things that weren't there because of the huge step she was taking. Putting everything behind her, the life she'd led, the worry she'd felt since deciding to follow through with her plan, she handed the driver her ticket and climbed on the bus. There was a seat in the very back, and she moved down the aisle toward it. After taking her seat, she glanced out the window and watched the cars passing by on the street. *Well, this is finally it. You're leaving all this shit behind.* That had a smile curving her mouth even if she felt scared shitless.

A tingling on the back of her neck had her turning away from the window and glancing at the front of the bus, and instantly her heart started to beat faster. The guy in the dark duster climbed aboard. His head was downcast, but he lifted his eyes and looked right at her. He took a seat a few rows in front of her, and she slid down in her seat so she could no longer see him, pulling the hood of her sweatshirt over her head. Exhaustion settled heavily inside of her and she knew she wouldn't be able to keep her eyes open much longer. Blissful ignorance as she slept and dreams of a happier place sounded a lot better than her reality.

Chapter Two

Ruby stepped off the bus and stretched. The sun was peeking over the buildings, and the smell of gas and smog filled her lungs. She stepped aside and allowed a few of the other riders to move past her. They had stopped several times throughout the night, but aside from a quick bathroom break and stretching her legs, Ruby had stayed on the bus. The man that initially made her feel uncomfortable was one of the first to disembark. The first thing she noticed was that he didn't have a bag with him. She hadn't even realized that when she had first seen him, but who went on a long trip like this without any kind of luggage? She had watched him through the window, saw him make his way toward a black stretch limo, get in, and then watched as it drove away. Why would he ride the Greyhound when he clearly had access to a limo? As he rode away in the limo, she put thoughts of him out of her head.

Inhaling the smoggy air wasn't pleasant, but she did feel freer. She walked over to a stack of newspapers, paid for one, and moved over to one of the plastic seats bolted to the ground. Ruby needed to find a place to sleep for a few nights until she found something more permanent. She had seen a stack of pamphlets, ones that had advertised less than attractive motels, but they had been in her price range—meaning dirt-cheap. She was starving, the morning weather was chilly, and the stops they had made along the way interrupted any sleep that she had gotten on the bus.

People were laughing and walking by, children were complaining about being hungry and tired—which she could relate to—and a small group of younger guys stood off to the side smoking cigarettes and speaking low. Ruby leaned over and grabbed a few of the pamphlets she had seen about the motels. She looked them over, not knowing exactly where to start, and feeling a little out of place. Truth be told, as excited as Ruby was to start this new chapter in her life, she felt lost inside of herself and more than a little afraid.

She had never felt like she belonged back home, never thought she was anything special, and certainly never made an impact on anyone. She went through each day in a repetitive motion. It worked for her, and she had chalked up her inner loneliness to the fact that her home life was anything but filled with the love and happiness that many families experienced.

Then there were the darker desires she had, the ones that invaded her dreams with pain and pleasure. She kept those desires hidden, never allowed them to control her, even though they tried. They were sick and twisted, and she knew they served no positive purpose in her life. Suddenly, Ruby became aware of the silence as people made their way from the bus station.

"Hey, pretty girl." The small group of guys walked over to her. There were three of them, and as she looked around, already knowing she was alone. She felt dread settle deep in her belly. She stood, feeling the weight of their stares on her as if they had physically reached out and taken hold of her. The bus had already pulled away, and a look in the small operator's box showed her that it was currently empty. Ruby's pulse increased and the flight or fight instinct moved through her with each step the guys took toward her.

"You shouldn't be all alone here. This isn't the best part of town," one of the guys said.

"I'm waiting for my boyfriend to come. He should be here any minute." The lie tumbled out of her easily, but the three guys chuckled and looked at each other.

"That right?" The guy in front of the other two stopped a few feet away and grinned. He lifted his cigarette to his mouth and inhaled deeply before blowing the smoke toward her. "How about we wait with you? Keep you company?"

She shook her head. "Not necessary, but thanks." Her throat felt tighter, her mouth very dry. He moved closer still, and the stench of stale cigarette smoke and sweat filled her nose. He reached out to touch her, but she took a step back. The bench behind her stopped her retreat, and his grin widened.

"The next bus won't be here for another half hour, and the asshole dishing out the tickets took a cigarette break just a second ago." He snagged a strand of her hair and gave it a hard enough tug that her head jerked to the side. "Girl, you got a mouth on you that was made to suck di—"

"Hey, punks, get the hell out of here." The deep, scratchy voice at her side had the three guys stepping away from her. "If I see you loitering around here again, I'm calling the cops." They turned, and all but ran in the other direction, and Ruby sagged in relief. She turned and looked at the guy that had saved her, realizing he must be the one they said went on a smoke break. He wore a uniform with the bus company's logo on it and had a cigarette hanging from between his lips. If he hadn't shown up when he did... she shook her head because she wasn't even about to go there.

"Kid, you better be careful. This is a shitty part of town, and not some place a young lady like you should be traveling alone, even if it is morning." She licked her lips and nodded. She bent down and picked up the paper, pamphlets, and her bag, before looking over at him again. He was probably in his fifties with a pot belly and a receding hairline.

"Thank you."

He nodded and looked down at the stack of papers she held. "If you're looking for a place to stay that is relatively decent, you can check out Liberty Inn. It's about a thirty-minute walk from here. Or a cab can take you, but some of the cabbies will try to rip you off." She nodded and offered him a wavering smile. Shouldn't afford a cab, and certainly not if she was jerked around with the price. Walking sounded much better after being on that bus all night anyway. "Just take a left at the intersection up there." He pointed to the main road off the bus station property. "Follow that all the way down until you see the donut shop with the giant freckled girl statue. Take a right and you can't miss it." He took a long puff from his cigarette. "It ain't the Hilton, but the sheets are clean and no one should bug you." She nodded and thanked him once more before she headed to the main road.

It took her longer than she would have liked to find the motel for the night, mainly because she had ended up getting turned around, even if the bus station attendant had given her pretty straightforward directions. Ruby was used to crowds, used to filth in her life. She was pretty sure the few women she had seen on the side of one street corner had been prostitutes, and the numerous homeless people that had been sitting in the corners of alleyways and against the sides of buildings had looked half-dead. She had known this city wasn't the best place to live, but it was big and had more job opportunities. She would travel tomorrow toward the better parts of the city, hoping to check out any positions she found in the classifieds.

She finally ended up finding the Liberty Inn, and it matched the scenery she had experienced thus far. It was a dump, plain and simple, but it had a roof and four walls, and the older woman at the front desk had been nice.

She tossed her bag on the floor and looked around the room. There was a full-sized bed in the center of the room with a brown and what she assumed was once white comforter. A TV that looked twenty years old sat on a scarred dresser across from the bed, and the bathroom was on the other side of the small hallway. She took the bag of fast food to the bed and sat down. Her mother would have realized she wasn't coming home, or maybe she was too drunk or high to notice. Either way, she'd know eventually that she was all alone now. Ruby knew that if her mother did care that she wasn't there, it was only because she wouldn't be getting any more money.

After she finished eating, she spread the paper out on the mattress and grabbed a pen. Looking over the classifieds didn't show much, mainly positions for which she wasn't qualified. However, she did see a couple secretary jobs, some positions for flipping burgers, and one for a maid. She circled all of them, set the stuff on the floor, and went over to the window.

The parking lot was riddled with potholes, and a few rusted cars and trucks sat in some of the spots. In the distance, she could see the tall buildings that made up Fort Hampton. She was about to close the drapes, when the sight of something flashing on the main road had her glancing that way. What she saw had her heart briefly stopping. A gleaming, black stretch limo sat across the street. Cars moved back and forth, partially obstructing her view, but she could clearly see the limo. Was it the same one from the bus station? The likelihood of that was slim, but Ruby couldn't help tingling of her skin as a strange sense of familiarity washed through her.

She closed the drapes and checked the locks on the door. Sleep sounded heavenly. She walked over to the bed and lay down. For several seconds she just stared at the cracked and water-stained ceiling, but soon her eyes grew heavy, and she submitted to the temptation of sleep.

A soft clicking sound woke Ruby. When she opened her eyes, the room was dark and she passed off the noise as a dream. She closed her eyes again, and soon the relaxation took hold once more. A noise right beside her, and the feeling of another presence in the room, had her eyes opening and her heart racing. Before she could react, there was a stinging pain in the side of her neck and a flash of fire following that.

She opened her mouth to scream, but someone clamped their hand over her mouth and nose. She struggled, God did she struggle, but even with her eyes wide open, she couldn't see a thing in the thick cloak of darkness. Flailing out her arms, hoping to connect with the intruder, she was able to slam her fist into the side of his face. There was a masculine grunt, and then he pressed his hand down harder on her mouth until her air supply was cut off and she was on the verge of passing out. She couldn't get any oxygen in, and it felt as though her heart would burst right through her chest. Then her limbs felt lead-filled, and her head felt separated from her body. This had nothing to do with the lack of oxygen, and everything to do with whatever he had injected into her neck. Right before the drug in her body completely claimed her, Ruby realized that her life might not have been so bad after all.

A jarring motion roused Ruby, and she tried to blink, but quickly realized something covered her eyes. Her head felt funny, her stomach roiled, and every muscle in her body ached. She tried to move her arms but they were bound behind her back, and when she tested her legs, she realized they were also in restraints.

Everything came rushing back to her, and as if her memories brought the pain back to the surface, her neck throbbed. Ruby took note of her surroundings, as much as she could with her senses diminished, and she knew instantly that she was in a vehicle. Given the fact she was laying on a hard metal ground, she assumed she was in a van or truck. She listened, but all she could hear was the vehicle moving. No one talked, so she didn't know how many people were in the vehicle with her. Although she couldn't see, while she knew someone was driving, she also knew there was someone else very close to her. That presence surrounded her, had fear slamming into her repeatedly like a sledgehammer, and had her feeling sick.

Sucking in a big lungful of air only caused her belly to cramp even more, and she knew she was going to throw up. Ruby rolled onto her side and emptied the contents of her stomach. There was shuffling beside her and she tensed when someone jerked her over and forced her to sit up. She could hear something opening before she felt something pressed to her mouth. Ruby turned her head, not knowing what they were trying to give her.

"You'd do good to behave." The voice was deep and slightly scratchy. Whoever spoke was right next to her, and he grabbed her chin harshly between his fingers and jerked her head back around. "It's water; now drink it." He pressed the bottle to her mouth again and tipped it back before she even had her mouth open. Some of the water got past her lips, but a lot of it spilled down her chin and covered her shirt. It went down the wrong tube and she coughed and gagged. She felt water spray out of her mouth, and when she heard the man curse, she knew she had spit it all over him. *Good, the bastard.* "You fucking cunt." Ruby braced herself for the hit that was inevitable, but another male voice, much sterner and filled with authority, came through.

"Don't lay a hand on her. You mark up the merchandise and the price decreases. You already bruised her jaw, you fucking idiot." The man beside her grumbled, but didn't harm her. He pushed her back down on the hard floor, and fear kept her immobile. She didn't know how long she lay there, keeping her mouth shut and just trying to listen to anything that would give her an idea of what was happening. Maybe she should have screamed, struggled more, but all she could think about was staying alive. After what seemed like hours, the vehicle pulled to a stop, and the doors opened and closed. There was a moment when all she heard was the sound of her frantic breathing. She felt the man's presence in the back with her and knew he was watching her despite the fact she couldn't see him.

"Where are you taking me?" Ruby had no idea where she actually got the strength to ask the question, but it had been tumbling around in her head, and apparently just spilled free. She clamped her mouth shut, expecting pain for speaking, but only heard silence. She felt the man's eyes on her, but he didn't respond, and her fear grew. "Are you going to hurt me?" It was a foolish question since they had already hurt her, but pain was a very real fear, as was the unknown, and she knew that they could cause so much more of it.

Her tears came out hard and strong, and their saltiness soon soaked the cloth that covered her eyes. The sound of deep murmurs right outside the vehicle was somewhat clear, but she could only grasp parts of what they were saying. She strained to hear more without looking like she was doing just that.

"She should fetch at least five digits. She's got a good body, decent face, pretty young. If she's still a virgin, that price will jump exponentially. She needs to be checked out thoroughly before we put her on the block."

The voice was muffled, but Ruby could hear him clear enough. It didn't take her long to realize what her fate was. She had seen enough shows about human sex trafficking to know that must be what they were talking about, and what they planned on doing with her. Something in her snapped, as fear, survival, and adrenalin pumped through her veins. She cried harder and started straining against her bonds, kicking out even though her legs were bound. She probably looked like a fish out of water, but she didn't care. All Ruby had on her mind was escape and survival.

Hands grabbed her upper arms, but she kept moving. She had to get out of here or she'd die. If this was her fate, then she wouldn't go down without a fight. Kicking both of her legs out again, Ruby renewed her strength and contacted with the man holding her down. She opened her mouth to scream, but the sound came out garbled. He smacked a hand down on her mouth hard enough that her eyes burned from the pain.

"You stupid fucking bitch."

She continued to struggle, but he moved his hand from her mouth to her throat and pressed down hard enough that she struggled to breathe. It was the same sensation she'd felt at the motel, and she tried to scream, even though no sound came out. With her hands tied behind her back, she was helpless, and her crying only made the suffocating feeling worse. He tightened his hand on her throat, and a low laugh came from him as she struggled. The sound of a door opening came through her distress, and suddenly she could breathe. Ruby sucked fresh, cool air into her burning lungs. Over her gasping, she heard the distinct sound of flesh hitting flesh. Seconds later, someone grabbed her bound feet and pulled. She cried harder and kicked out, but whoever had her jerked even harder until she was no longer in the van, but on the hard ground. The air whooshed out of her from the impact, and then, violently hauled upright, her head was tugged back by the hair, and then someone gripped her chin and turned her head from side to side. A moment of silence passed.

"Decent body, if on the thin side, but she'll look good with the others on the stage."

"Please, just let me go." No one spoke after that, instead she was thrust forward and into the arms of another man. "Please, just let me go home," Ruby cried, begged and pleaded, but there was silence. "I won't say anything to anyone, I swear."

"Little girl, your home will be with whoever purchases you." That had her blood chilling and her body tensing. She had assumed as much, but actually hearing it aloud made it solidify inside of her. There was a low, sadistic chuckle. "That's right. Your life is over; you are just an object up for bid." Before she could say anything else there was another sting in her neck, but this time the drug slammed into her fast and hard.

"Put her in the cargo hold with the others."

That was the last thing she heard before she slumped forward and darkness was her only companion.

Chapter Three

Ruby hung her head and shuffled forward with the other women. She didn't know where she was or how long she had been in captivity. Time had run together until she didn't know if it had been days, or even weeks. All she knew was that after she had woken up the second time she no longer had the blindfold on, but was now bound and gagged, in what appeared to be a storage compartment of a plane, with a handful of other women, all similarly restrained, crammed inside.

After what felt like hours on the airplane, they finally landed. Blindfolded, they were hauled out as if they were nothing but worthless cargo. They moved all the women to one large room with no windows, only one guarded exit, and a hole in the ground to be used as their toilet. They slept on stained and nasty-smelling mattresses on the floor, ate disgusting food that didn't even look edible, drank brown-tinted water, and washed in a communal shower room. The men that stood guard over them never touched or hurt them; they just barked orders as if they were dogs. They had taken her away once, drugged her, and restrained her to a table. But she had blacked out after that. She didn't know what they had done to her and had woken up back on the disgusting mattress in the room with the other women. Images of them touching her while she was unconscious, of violating her had played through her mind. She hadn't felt any differently, wasn't sore, but she couldn't shake off the feeling that they had done something very wrong to her.

Even now, as she slowly moved forward in line, all she could remember was hearing the screams of one of the girls that had dared to speak out. She had scratched and kicked at one of the men until they had taken her away, away form Ruby and the rest of the women. It had seemed like forever before they'd brought her back. When they did, Ruby knew that whatever they had done to her had broken a part of her. She had a distant look in her eyes, an almost lost expression. It was one of the most frightening things Ruby had ever seen.

Maybe Ruby should have fought harder, tried to connect with the other girls held captive, but they were always watched, ordered to stay silent, and the fear of her situation and of pain kept her silent. She felt weak, cowardly, even though she knew she had simply been trying to stay alive. Conflict ran high inside of her, the tug and pull of doing something to retaliate, or being meek and submissive to survive. They didn't hit her, and for that, she was thankful, but the words she had heard when she was first taken played in her head repeatedly.

"You mark up the merchandise and the price decreases."

So she stayed quiet, did as she was told, and knew that this wasn't her last stop. There had been enough cryptic conversations from the men guarding them that Ruby understood they would be sold, even if she hadn't already come to that conclusion the very first night of her capture. To who they were being sold was still a mystery, but Ruby had seen enough documentaries on the depraved things that would be forced upon her ran through her head like a horrifying movie reel.

Now here she stood, in a line wearing nothing but a shift with a rope binding her wrists together in front of her. She glanced up and saw a thick curtain blocking her view of their ultimate destination. Everything was silent aside from the few girls that were sniffling back their tears. She looked to the side and saw the men on each side of the line that had their eyes trained on them. Ruby shivered from the chill in the air especially since she wore a very loose fitting shift that looked more like a pillowcase than an actual dress. It was clean though, and all the women had been forced to wash very thoroughly right before they bound and gagged them once more and thrust them into the back of a van.

A man stepped out from behind the curtain. She had never seen him before, but he looked like he had money. Maybe he was the one that controlled this entire sick operation. He wore an expensive-looking suit, a shining gold watch, and had a diamond stud in his ear. He looked far too old to be wearing an earring, maybe even closer to her grandfather's age, but there was a very cold expression on his face as he looked over each girl in line. He didn't say anything at first, and when he had looked at all of them, he moved back to the curtain and clasped his hands in front of him. For several seconds, all he did was stand there, and a few of the girls started crying harder.

"This is your last stop, children," he said, and while those words held a lot of meaning, they were cryptic. The older man tilted his chin to someone, and the men on either side of them stepped forward. In the blink of an eye, they produced needles and proceeded to inject each girl. The ones that realized what was happening struggled at first in surprise and then fear, no doubt. However, whatever they injected them with worked fast and soon the women were making low sounds and slumping forward. Whatever was in those needles couldn't have been too strong, though, because the girls were able to remain standing. All of this happened within seconds, and Ruby turned and glanced at the man now moving toward her.

"Please, I'll do whatever you say; I don't need that." He didn't even meet her eyes, instead snatched her arm in a firm grasp, stabbed the needle into her, and depressed the plunger. A burning sensation started at the point of contact, and tears formed in the corner of her eyes.

"You need to behave, and to appeal to the bidders, hence the little chemical persuasion we gave you." The old man spoke without a hint of remorse, but then Ruby didn't expect any person that was involved with kidnapping and selling women would have any morals or empathy.

She started to feel lightheaded, felt her arms become too heavy to hold up, and weaved slightly. She had been drunk once in her life, and the effects were similar, but more pronounced, more relaxed, and she knew that right now they were nothing more than droids for these men. She could still think clearly. But it seemed like it took a very long time for her mind to process that information.

The first few girls were pushed forward. There was a shove from behind her and she stumbled into the girl in front of her. Her mouth became unbearably dry, and her tongue felt thick. She couldn't stop the tears, couldn't even force herself to do anything but put one foot in front of the other. Shaking her head to try and clear it only made the room spin and her stomach churn. A few steps led up to the curtained-off area, and once she cleared those, she stepped onto a platform. Lights beamed down, and she had to close her eyes momentarily from the harsh glare. Ruby tried to lift her arms again, but they were just too heavy, and every step she took felt like she was trying to move through thick mud. When the girl in front of her stopped, hands grabbed Ruby's arms and moved her into the position they wanted. She tried to cover herself, even if she was wearing the god-awful dress, but she couldn't find the strength. She wore no undergarments under the gown and knew her nipples and the small patch of her pubic hair were clearly visible through the paper-thin material. Although she didn't hear anything aside from the occasional shuffling sound, she felt so many eyes on her that a light sweat started to form along her forehead. No one spoke, but each girl, starting at the front of the line, was pushed forward for a few seconds, and then immediately pulled back, as if they had been discarded. Ruby turned and glanced sideways, trying to see, but her vision would not focus.

Each time a girl was pushed forward, the older man would state their age and whether they were a virgin or not. There were more non-virgins than there were virgins. When they got to the girl beside her, Ruby watched as she curled into herself and started to cry harder. The old man whispered something harsh to her, and she looked up at him with wide eyes. Everything was so fuzzy that she could see his mouth moving, but couldn't make out the hushed words he said. Whatever they were had the girl crying harder and shaking her head in response. He yanked her forward, deemed her a non-virgin, and pushed her back in line as if he couldn't stand to touch her. Then it was her turn, and all the strength that Ruby had thought she had vanished when he wrapped a wrinkled hand around her arm, grinned down at her, and pulled her forward.

Gavin Darris leaned back in his chair and stared at each young woman presented. There were about ten other men sitting in the crudely erected auction room. Although this certainly wasn't a luxurious setting, he was here for the merchandise, not the scenery. The items up for sale were young women, barely legal girls really. Gavin knew they had been taken from their homes against their will and were being offered up like cattle to a pack of wolves. He should have felt disgusted with himself for being here, but he wasn't, and in fact had been eagerly waiting for this night for the past month when he'd found out about it. Having an unlimited amount of wealth and knowing very corrupt men made finding and visiting these little auctions very easy.

There was a wide variety of females on the stage, all wearing the same white sheet-like dress, and having the same drugged expression. But they ranged in age, race, hair color, and body type. Gavin wasn't particularly picky on the submissive he wanted, but what he craved was a woman that was his fully. He wasn't in need of female company, didn't want someone to chat with. What he wanted was a woman that didn't give herself to him because of his social status or bank account. He wanted a true submissive in every word, not one he found at a club. He wasn't particularly fond of the BDSM club scene. He wanted a submissive that would learn to enjoy having his marks on her body, a woman that would writhe and crave his touch when he restrained her, and gave her pain.

Gavin needed the total control that a female could give him, that a masochist could give him. He didn't want their surrender because the female thought to gain something in return, but one that needed to unleash the inner pain as much as he did.

Purchasing a kidnapped female who had been drugged was certainly not the most honorable thing a man could do, but then Gavin had never claimed to be anything of the sort. He was who he was, had a limitless bank account to purchase a harem of submissives if he chose, but all he wanted was one that would look at him like he held her very life in his hands. And he would, in every sense of the word.

Each female was presented to the silent bidders, and out of the corner of his eye, he saw hands being raised as bids were placed. These human auctions were always at different, secluded spots where only a few select people knew about them. Gavin couldn't say why he had chosen this particular one when he had known about countless ones before. He had just known that it was time to put away the countless women he had fucked who had tried to be submissive, tried to find one the traditional way, and would now get one the unconventional way. So far no female piqued his interest, tempted the dark bastard inside of him.

And then he saw *her*, and everything in him stilled.

She swayed on her feet, and her tears were a continuous flow down her cheeks. Her tears had his dick hardening and the sadistic asshole inside of him growing excited. The light shone through her gown, and the sight of her dark pubic hair and hard nipples and areolas had his cock throbbing. Her hair was long, wavy, and a dark brown. Even from the short distance and through the drugged-out expression of her half-lidded and red-rimmed eyes, he could see the very vibrant green of her irises. Gavin shifted and leaned forward, trying to get a better look at her, but there was no denying that he wanted her, and that she would be the one that would sate his dark, primal urges.

"Eighteen-year-old certified virgin," the man presenting the woman announced as he pulled the brunette forward. Where she had been timid and stayed in line with the others just moments before, something snapped behind her eyes when the older gentleman ran his hand down her back. He pulled the material of the shift back until it tightened on the front of her body. Her breasts pressed against the fabric in all their glory, and he got an unobstructed view of her slender form. She had curves, but her legs where long and toned, and her belly flat. Her breasts were also large for her size, but she was perfect, and he was certain when he saw a determined and fierce expression cover her face.

Gavin watched curiously, as she started to struggle. She lifted her bound hands, tried to bring them down on the man that held her. When that didn't work, she strained forward, the fear and need to escape clear on her face. But her movements were slow from whatever they had clearly given her. The older man's face took on a red hue. Hands in the bidding area started to lift. A fighter wasn't what every man here wanted, but it excited more than a handful. The kind of people that came to these auctions—men like himself—clearly liked the darker pleasures in life. He didn't need to look into their eyes to see the depravity of their desires, of their need to break and ruin her, remold her into whatever pet they saw fit. But Gavin wanted to give her pleasure and pain as much as he took it, and no one in this dammed place would stop him from getting her.

Chapter Four

After they stood on the platform for several minutes, they were ushered back behind the curtain once more. Ruby expected to be punished for her little outburst on the stage, and honestly, she didn't know what had gotten into her. But when that guy had pulled on her dress, showing off her body like it was free to be seen, she had just lost it. She didn't want this, had sat by idly, and behaved like she was this little victim long enough for the sake of surviving, but she just couldn't do it anymore.

"Girl, you're lucky someone purchased you. If not, I would have made sure you paid for that little show with blood." Ruby started to shake uncontrollably as the old man leaned in close and grinned. "But I know you will spill enough blood with your owner to appease my thoughts." He gripped her arm and pushed her forward to one of the guards. "Get her cleaned up." These bastards were selling them as if they were nothing more than inanimate objects. She was a human being, but treated as something that could just be purchased from the store. She knew she would experience pain, degradation, and vile things at the hand of her owner. There was no beautiful illusion that whoever purchased her would let her go, or at the very least treat her like she was an actual person.

No, this person would be sick and abusive, perverted, with nightmarish delusions that they could do whatever they wanted to her. How could they be any different if they were buying a woman?

How could she escape when she didn't even know where she was? But she would much rather die trying than survive as someone's sexual slave. Bile rose in her throat at the thought of someone actually thinking they owned her.

Owner. She was no one's property, and would make that clear, even if it was with her last breath.

Her handler took her over to a row of other women Ruby assumed had been purchased as well. She looked over at the other handful of girls, and the sick feeling in her stomach intensified when she saw them being herded out the back door. She didn't know what their fate held, but she hoped it was better than hers was, although she realized how foolish that thought was as soon as it came to her.

They had already showered before the auction, so she wasn't sure what they planned to do next. They were led into a small room, and Ruby looked around. There were a few vanities and a few young women standing by them. The guy behind her pushed her toward one of the seats. He shoved her down on it and took a few steps back when the woman came forward. She didn't speak or make eye contact with Ruby. She wondered if this was a kidnapped woman that hadn't been bought. Ruby's hair was brushed and left down, lotion was applied to her exposed skin, and a floral perfume was applied to her pulse points. She didn't fight, because the drugs were thick in her, and she had a hard time focusing. This felt like some kind of grotesque episode of behind the scenes of a sex-trafficking auction. The other girls in the room were quiet, but when Ruby glanced at them, she saw silent tears rolling down their cheeks.

"Please, I need your help." Ruby said in a whisper and stared into the woman's face. She couldn't be more than twenty, but there was an age around her eyes and mouth that spoke of a life lived a hundred times over. There was no reaction from the woman, so Ruby tried again. She had to, because once she was back in the hands of these men, they would haul her away and the nightmare that was now her life would start. "Please, please look at me." There was a flicker in the woman's dark eyes. The girl moved to the side of her, blocking the view of the door.

"You must be quiet or we will both be in trouble." The young woman had a thick accent, maybe from South America. She ran the brush through her hair once more. Ruby looked at the table where make-up and brushes were laid out. Before she could say anything else to the woman, or plead with her, she was hauled out of the chair and pushed out of the room with everyone else. Ruby's heart pounded hard and fast, and beads of perspiration started to dot her forehead. They had bound her hands after her shower earlier, and the rope dug into her flesh. She was led toward a different door at the end of a long hallway, and when it was opened, she saw that it was dark outside. A cool breeze whistled by, moving the tendrils of her hair from her shoulder, and sending chills through her body.

A dark limo sat a few feet away, and a wave of déja vu slammed into her. Was the man that bought her the same one that she had seen on the bus and then watched get into the limo back in Fort Hampton? That didn't seem very likely since he could have just taken her without having to go through all of this trouble.

An older man climbed out of the driver's side and walked around to open the back passenger door. He didn't speak, didn't even look at her. She was led forward again, but she was tremendously scared at what was inside the dark confines of that vehicle. She couldn't see anything aside from a pair of legs encased in what looked like a suit, and black, shiny dress shoes. Ruby's tongue was so thick she thought she would choke on it. Every step she took felt like she was one step closer to meeting her executioner. She started struggling once more, although she knew it wouldn't make any difference now; she couldn't go willingly.

"Please, God, *please* let me go." She'd been unrestrained, and she tugged and pulled at the two men holding onto her arms, heard their grunts as they struggled with her, and although there was no way she could overpower them, she tried. But everything inside of her stilled when a hand slowly emerged from the interior of the car, palm up, and fingers curling inward like he was trying to coax her forward. That small moment of stunned fear at seeing that masculine hand with those long, strong-looking fingers seeming to reach for her, was enough of a pause for her captors to pull her forward and push her onto the floor of the limo. The door slammed shut behind her and she scrambled off the ground and onto the seat. Pushing herself against the side of the car, she heard the locks engage and stared with horror at the man seated across from her.

He wore a dark, expensive three-piece suit. The small part of the shirt underneath was a stark white and the tie a light blue— the same color as his cold, bottomless eyes. He appeared to be very muscular, and that strength wasn't hidden behind the material of his clothing. With his long, muscular limbs, Ruby had no doubt he could crush her with little thought. Suddenly, she couldn't breathe as the air inside of the vehicle grew warmer, and the scent of his spicy, intoxicating cologne filled her head.

"Breathe." She snapped her eyes up to his face when he spoke. His voice was a deep timbre; that one word held a lot of power. She sucked in lungful after lungful of oxygen, and a sardonic smile covered his face, as if he was pleased that she had listened with no fight. "Tell me your name." She shook her head, her throat closed, and she started to shake uncontrollably. "Relax, darling." He smiled, and she was sure he had used that on countless people to make them do his bidding, but to her he just looked like a predator. She didn't want to show this reaction in front of him, but she couldn't help it.

Maybe she was in shock? Yes, that had to be it, because if this didn't throw someone into a state of shock she didn't know what would. Instead, she tried to gain control of herself. Licking her lips only had him looking down at her mouth and watching the act. "Where are you taking me?" The car started to move and Ruby brought her knees to her chest, adjusted the shift to cover herself, and wrapped her arms around her legs.

"To your new home." A chill froze her as she heard those words leave his perfect mouth. The devil took on a very beautiful form, but underneath he was still a horrible, evil creature. He watched her silently after that, with the corner of his mouth slightly turned up. No doubt, he enjoyed her discomfort and fear.

His dark hair was short and perfectly styled. There wasn't a hair out of place, or a stitch of his perfectly tailored suit disheveled. This was a man in control, and one that held a lot of power. She didn't want to look at him, didn't want to see that the monster that had bought her was a beautiful demon. Her shitty life back with her mother in that rundown trailer didn't look so bad right now, even though wealth surrounded her, and the man that "owned" her was stunningly handsome. She looked away, buried her face against her knees, and prayed to whoever might be listening that she would wake up and this would all be one horrifying, screwed-up nightmare.

Gavin watched her look around the foyer of his home—of *her* new home. The limo ride from the auction had been a long three-hour ride. Then they had taken his private jet to his European estate in the countryside. It was isolated, with the nearest town hours away. It was the perfect place to keep his new purchase, especially since he knew she would be trying to run.

"You like your new home?" He stayed by the door and watched her. Her feet were bare, and she still wore that God-awful shift, but he'd remedy that soon enough. She looked over at him but didn't respond. In fact, she hadn't said one word since she had asked where they were going. Her fear was understandable, and he didn't expect her to bend to his will instantly, but she would eventually. Gavin was a patient man in some respects, but when it concerned this brunette, his property, he had many deliciously twisted things he wanted to do to her, and he wouldn't wait forever to experience them.

She wrapped her arms around her middle and turned to face him completely. "This isn't my home." He smiled, but he was grappling for control right now. She hadn't uttered more than a few words to him on the very long journey to his estate, not even when he had tried to get her to open up to him on the plane; it had annoyed him as much as it tempted the monster inside of him to make her tell him everything about herself.

Of course, he wasn't talking about a literal monster inside of him, but there were days when he felt as though the evil and darkness were stronger than he was. Purchasing her had been a very good idea, but also a very bad idea. He regretted nothing, though, and his actions were always calculated.

"Princess, this is the only home you will ever know from this point forward." He heard her swallow, saw her throat move up and down from the act, and saw the slight tremble in her body.

"Do you plan on hurting me? Will you rape me?" She started crying, and his dick punched forward. He was a sick, sadistic bastard for deriving pleasure from her clear pain, but he'd teach her that with pain came pleasure. The end result would be a coupling to rival all others, and one that could never be broken. Because for him, this female was his in any way he wanted.

He didn't move, didn't try to hide his arousal from her, and when he saw her look at his crotch and her eyes widen, he was satisfied that she was clearly frightened by the sight. He was a big man... all over.

"Please."

His heart pounded faster at that one word, and in his mind he could picture her on her knees, her tears falling fast as she looked up at him and begged him to stop, but would then plead for him to continue.

"Say it again." His words came out as a low and harsh, and she took a step back.

"W-What?"

He took a step forward. "Say that word again."

The pulse at the base of her neck beat frantically, and she swallowed again. "*Please.*"

It took a lot of self-control on his part not to go to her, rip off her clothes, and fuck her right there on the stairs, but there would be plenty of time for that. He might be a bastard, but he wasn't a savage. She needed to bathe and eat, and he was sure she was exhausted. Of course, she would have a slew of questions, and he had answers, whether she liked them or not.

This man, whose name she didn't even know, had led her up the spiraling staircase, down a short ornate hallway, and gestured for her to enter a room. Ruby had never been this frightened in her life, not even when one of her mother's boyfriends had come into her room late one night and tried to touch her. After a swift kick to his balls, she had vowed to never be a victim again. But clearly she had broken her own promise to herself at the first major disaster in her life. She shouldn't have left, and should have just lived the life she had been dealt. Maybe she was being punished? She had never been an overly religious person, but she liked to believe in heaven and hell, and thought that with evil there was always good. Had she done something wrong? She had stolen some nail polish from a convenience store when she was thirteen because her mom refused to buy it for her. Maybe this was karma making its way around all these years later? Although she certainly wouldn't have considered that a life-changing sin, maybe that was all it took for someone to learn their lesson.

She stepped into the opulent room and was struck by the beauty of it right away. The shades were a soft silvery color and light blue. The rest of the room was made up of lace accents and dainty furniture. The trip to get to this massive home had been long, and she couldn't deny that she was happy finally to be on solid ground. She had no clue where she was, but she had seen the vast ocean below them from the jet, and knew wherever she was, it was far away from where she'd started. They hadn't landed at an airport, and there hadn't been any kind of security asking them for legal documentation to get into the country. In fact, the plane had landed in a hangar, and then a car had brought them to this place just a few minutes away. Ruby had been on alert to her surroundings, and to her utter disappointment, she had only seen miles and miles of land as far as she could see.

"You'll clean up and dress for dinner." She turned and looked at him, but fear closed off her throat and swelled her tongue. At that moment, she couldn't have responded even if he had asked her something directly. She didn't know what he had planned, but it seemed she had the rest of her life to figure it out. Whatever this evil bastard was going to do to her would surely not be something that she would ever want. He was holding her prisoner, probably keeping her here to be his little sex slave. Why else would a man have to purchase a woman? But he was gorgeous in his own right; why would he need to resort to buying someone that had been kidnapped? Nevertheless, all she had to do to feel the darkness in him was look in his blue eyes. They almost seemed void of life, and she had glimpsed another presence within him. She had a sickening realization that this was only the very beautiful surface of a monster.

She didn't say anything, just stared at him. He had a very stoic expression, but she wasn't fooled into thinking his guard was down in the slightest. There he stood in his dark suit with his hands behind his back and his feet slightly parted. He looked very intimidating, controlled, and like he had everything planned out. But of course he did.

"There are clothes your size in the armoire and dresser, and the bathroom is over there." He pointed at a closed door to his left. "You are old enough to clean and dress yourself, but I have two servants that are here at all times to tend to the house. If you need anything you have but to ask." He slowly let his eyes move up and down her body, and she crossed her arms over her chest when she felt her nipples harden. She was far from aroused, but the sight of him was almost as powerful as if he was reaching out and actually touching her. "I'm sure you have a lot of questions, but those will be answered later. Right now, you're filthy, and I want you clean and looking presentable." She swallowed at his words. "You are my property, Princess, and as such will obey any and everything I say. That is the first rule." He took a step closer, and she moved one back. This dark look covered his face, and he shook his head. "The second rule is that you never deny me." He stopped in front of her, but she had nowhere to go anyway. The bed was behind her, and no way in hell was she going to get on that just to get away from him. He would probably take that as an invitation to use her body, and that was not going to happen.

"Do you plan on hurting me?" she asked again since he hadn't answered her the first time. Again, he didn't respond right away, but instead lifted his hand. Ruby tensed and watched as he moved that hand closer to her.

He lifted a piece of her hair off her shoulder and looked at it, rubbing it between his fingers. He slowly moved his gaze away from her hair and looked at her face. "You are very pretty. Very beautiful, in fact." He said the words low and deep as he looked in her eyes, but she wasn't fooled by this seemingly gentle disposition. This man was a demon intent on hurting her.

"Will you hurt me?" Ruby asked again. She would continue to do so until he answered her.

He titled his head slightly to the side and seemed to study her. "Tell me your name." She shook her head. She wouldn't give any part of herself to him. Not one damn part. When she didn't answer, he moved the hand that held her hair to her throat. It was a loose hold, but the threat was there. He could have snapped her neck, or strangled her without breaking a sweat. "Have you forgotten the rules already, Princess? Obey everything I say." He lifted a dark eyebrow, but otherwise kept a very hard composure. "Now, I will only ask you once more, and if you disobey, I promise you will not like my reaction."

Ruby felt sweat bead her forehead, knew her eyes were as big as saucers, and felt the strength she had wanted to hold onto crumble. She was weak, so frightened of what he would do, that she opened her mouth to give him what he wanted.

"Ruby Jacobson." As soon as her name left her lips, she felt like a failure. She had given him what he wanted so easily. What else would she give him without much of a fight? The corner of his mouth lifted, and a very pleased look crossed his face.

"Good girl." He moved his hand up the side of her throat until he could brush his thumb along her bottom lip. But everything inside of her was frozen. "And to answer your question..." He didn't say anything for several seconds after that, and she knew it was to make her think about that statement, to make her fear him more, and it certainly had the desired effect. "Yes, Ruby, I do plan on hurting you." Then he leaned down and took her mouth with his own. It started off slowly at first, but he became more demanding and rough with his lips, teeth, and tongue. She placed her hands on his chest, felt the hard, defined muscles flex beneath her touch, and pushed him away, or at least tried to. He was very strong, so much stronger than she was. She was able to push him away, but only because he allowed her to. She covered her mouth with her hands, felt the blood rush to the surface of her lips from where he had lightly bitten her sensitive flesh, and couldn't stop herself from crying.

"I can be a lenient man, Ruby, and treat you as a treasured pet, but my patience can only go so far, especially if you are adamant on being stubborn and denying me what is rightfully mine." He spoke the words evenly, but she wasn't fooled into thinking he was calm in the slightest. His erection tented the front of his pants, and she cried harder. That only made him grin. "And just so you know, seeing you cry makes me even more turned on, darling."

She dropped her hand and said in a wavering voice, "I'm not yours, and never will be. You don't own me even if you bought me." She gripped her gown as soon as the words had left her. She was pushing him, she knew this, but she couldn't just stand here, let him touch her, kiss her, and speak to her as if she was nothing but an object that he could fuck any way he wanted to.

"That is where you are wrong, Ruby."

She licked her lips again. Had she spoken that aloud?

"You *are* something. In fact, you're something very special to me, Princess." He reached out and smoothed a finger along her jawline, and she couldn't move as he touched her. Then he moved away from her, turned, and left, shutting the door behind him. There was no click from him locking the door and so she moved closer, gripped the handle, and turned it.

To her shock, it opened silently. She glanced out into the hallway and saw him descending the stairs, but he stopped right before he disappeared past the banister and turned to look at her. "This is your home. You're not a prisoner, but you are mine. Let there be no mistake that there is any escape because I won't let you go. The sooner you come to terms with that the sooner you can start to accept your new life and enjoy it." He stared at her for a long moment, and she gripped the handle tighter to stop her shaking hand. "And don't make me have to come back up and fetch you, Ruby."

He turned and left her standing there. Ruby stepped back into the room and closed the door. She rested both hands on the smooth, cool wood and leaned her forehead against it, closing her eyes. That last parting statement had been a threat and a dark promise. She had heard that although he didn't want her to disobey him, part of him relished the idea of her disobedience. That had been clear when the corner of his mouth lifted and he flared his nostrils, excited.

Ruby turned and pushed away from the door and looked at her beautiful prison. Everything was cleaned to perfection, and the sweet smell of something akin to flowers and baby powder filled her nose. She walked over to the window and pushed the heavy drapes aside. She was too far up to try and escape that way, and although she probably would have survived a fall, she wasn't in the mood for broken bones. The scenery was quite breathtaking, with flat, green land long and far in the distance, thin, willowy trees on either side of the house, and the promise of freedom just beyond the glass and stone of her prison.

Moving away from the window, she walked toward the armoire and after taking a deep breath, reached out and grabbed the ornately yet daintily carved brass handles. Pulling open the doors revealed an array of shoes, mainly stilettos, evening and casual gowns, skirts, and blouses. All were silky, lacy, and very feminine. And all in her size... scarily enough. She turned and opened the drawers of the dresser and found satin slips, hose and garter belts. Amidst all the articles of clothing were two things that were very much absent. Bras and panties. Clearly, he liked to have his playthings easily accessible to his depravity. She slammed the drawers shut as hard as she could and got a small moment of pleasure from that act of rebellion.

Ruby needed to decide if she was going to fight this with tooth and nail, risk whatever wrath was hidden behind the gorgeous exterior of her captor, or fold and play the perfect piece of property that he clearly wanted. She sat on the edge of the bed and stared at the bedroom door. He was just downstairs, and the threat of not making him come "fetch" her played in her mind constantly. She was good at thinking about the horrible things he would do to her, and they weren't things she wanted to see come true. So she stood, walked over to the closet, and grabbed the first thing she touched. She went into the bathroom, turned the light on, but wasn't surprised to see this also held a wealth of opulence. What she did know was that right now, she might concede to what he wanted, but she would fight for her freedom and would find a way out of this place.

Wherever they were was very far from civilization, but it didn't take a genius to realize why he would want to be isolated from everyone and everything. If no one could hear her scream, then no one would come for her. But there was no one to come for her anyway. She had no real friends, no family that gave a shit about her. No one. She was just another statistic and soon she would be forgotten, if, in fact, she'd ever been thought about at all.

Chapter Five

Gavin sat across from Ruby at the dining room table and watched her. She looked very uncomfortable, which was evident by the way she kept fidgeting. "Wouldn't you like to know my name? Or anything else about me?" She glanced up at him, but didn't respond. It amused him, but his humor only went so far.

She shook her head, but there was a spark of fire in her eyes. "I don't care who you are. All I know is you're holding me against my will."

He smirked at her little outburst. "I suppose, but your life here will be very comfortable. You will never want for anything." She stared at him, and although she tried to keep her face blank, he saw the way she clamped her jaw.

"All the money in the world wouldn't make me want to stay here with you."

Gavin was trying to stay calm, but no one spoke to him this way, least of all a woman. She must have seen the dark look move over his face because her lips parted and she breathed out forcefully enough that he heard her. Ruby didn't say anything else, which was very smart of her, and Gavin let himself relax once more.

"Ask me, Ruby." She glanced down, but before he could order her to keep her eyes on him, she was looking at him once more. "Ask about the man that owns every part of you." She was so very young, but she had a strength that rivaled his own. It had been that strength that made him want her so badly even if he wanted her to surrender it to him in the end. He wanted a woman that would fight him, would give as good as she could take, and he knew Ruby was that woman.

"I don't know what to ask." He clenched his jaw. This felt like tug and pull with a child. But she started speaking again. "What's your name? How old are you? Where am I and how long do you plan on keeping me here? What do you do since it is clear you're wealthy enough to buy a stolen human being? And why do you feel you even need to buy a woman?" She rambled off the questions, and although she was attempting to sound genuine, there was no doubt in his mind that she was trying to show her stubborn will. But she would realize that he was the only dominant one in this coupling. She asked that last question quickly as if she had been slightly unsure if she wanted to tread that territory once more. He let it slide though. This was her first night, and he could be a lenient man, but she would follow his rules, and if she thought she could break them after that, well, he looked forward to delivering a very delicious punishment.

"My name is Gavin Darris. You are at my home in Europe, far, *far* away from civilization." He grinned at her, making her aware that if she thought of escaping she wouldn't get very far in finding someone to help her. "And I plan on keeping you here for a *very* long time, Ruby." He ran his finger along his napkin but kept his focus on her. "My work doesn't concern you, aside from the point that occasionally I must travel, and when that is the case you will stay here. I'm thirty-seven, and no, I don't need to purchase women, but just because I don't need to doesn't mean I don't want to." She kept running her finger along her fork, and he saw the slight tremble in her hand.

"Am I the first woman you've purchased, or do you have a harem stashed somewhere in this house?" He could tell by her voice that she wasn't trying to fight with him on this question. She was truly curious.

"You are the first woman I have ever purchased. And the last." Her eyes widened slightly. Gavin watched her run her tongue along the swell of her bottom lip, and his cock, which had gotten instantly hard when he saw her enter the dining room, grew harder still.

"Can you at least tell me what you plan on doing with me?"

"Don't be foolish. You know exactly what I plan to do with you. Why else would a man purchase a woman from an auction if not to enjoy her body?" He lifted his wine glass to his lips and took a long swallow while watching her over the rim. She picked up her fork and started moving the food around her plate. "You don't like the grilled salmon?" She glanced up at him, but quickly averted her eyes. "I asked you a question, Ruby." She looked up at him again and set her fork down.

"No, in fact I don't." He knew she probably meant to sound stronger, but those words came out in a whisper.

"You don't like seafood?" He wiped his mouth with the linen napkin and set it down. Gavin leaned back in his seat and wrapped his fingers around the stem of his wine glass.

"Being kidnapped and held captive has a way of ruining a person's appetite."

He cocked an eyebrow. "Yes, I suppose it does." He stared at her for several seconds. She started to fidget again. "Do I make you nervous?" She looked at him with shock written across her face, although it was a rhetorical question because he knew he did. She didn't answer, but once again looked down at her lap. "Look at me, Ruby." She didn't, and he slammed his fist down on the table, knocking over his wine glass. The chardonnay spilled across the white tablecloth, but his focus was on the young woman across from him. She was now looking at him, her eyes wide and her back pressed all the way against the back of the chair. Gavin leaned in and rested his forearms on the table. "Since my politeness in starting a civil conversation is not going over the way it should, I will just have to do this the hard way." She audibly swallowed. "This is your new home, Ruby. You are mine, my property, to do with as I please. I have certain desires, and you are the one that will appease them." She started shaking her head, but he didn't think she even realized she was doing it. "Oh yes, Princess. I have many things planned for you, for your body, and how to make you scream for more."

"I will never want that, or you." Her voice shook as she spoke.

"We will see, darling."

"Why me?" Fat tears fell from her eyes and she angrily wiped them away. He leaned back again and smiled. "Why can't you just tell me that? You can tell me everything else, but have yet to tell me why you are really keeping me here."

He had told her already why she was here—to pleasure him. But it was clear his earlier words were not getting through to her. He knew her fear was paramount, knew that this must be very hard for her, but she would have to get used to it and accept it.

"Why not you? You were there for the taking, sweet Ruby. But I saw something special in you, something fiery and determined. I knew when you struggled on that stage that I had to have you for myself. I liked the fighter I saw in you, and there wasn't anyone that would stop me from what I wanted, and what I wanted was you." She didn't respond for several seconds. "Go on, Ruby, tell me how you feel."

Normally he wouldn't have cared what a woman thought. He also didn't care what others thought if he didn't directly ask them. That was the way of the world, of his business, and it suited him fine. But Ruby was different than the others. Yes, he owned her, and yes, she would be the perfect pet for his deliciously sadistic pleasures. But he just needed to look in her eyes to know that her resistance would slowly fade as she came to terms with her life now. It would take time, but they had an abundance of that.

"You do realize how wrong this is?" He thought about what she had just asked, but all he could do was smile. "You do realize I was kidnapped, drugged, and sold like cattle?" She had stopped crying, and once again, he saw that flash of fire behind her eyes.

"None of that matters, Ruby, because you are here now, and I have no intention of letting you go. But if it makes you feel better, you are more than welcome to tell me your dreams and aspirations." He smiled wider as he saw the way she bunched her hands into fists on the table.

"It doesn't matter anyway."

"Oh, but it does. I'd like to know about you, Princess."

"Stop calling me that."

His former easygoing attitude started to fade at her words. "You don't make the demands, I do." His voice was low, and he slammed his fist on the table once again. She jumped, and he liked that she was frightened of him. "I'll call you anything that pleases me. You are here for *my* enjoyment. If I choose to give you pleasure, then you greedily accept it, say thank you, and hope I am generous enough to give you more."

She stood quickly, knocking her chair over in the process. She was shaking her head and glancing around the room for an exit, but she wouldn't get far. She took off toward the door that led into the kitchen, but he was already out of his seat and striding toward her. He pushed the kitchen door open with so much force it slammed against the opposite wall. She cried out and spun around, and in her fear and haste to get away, she knocked over the serving wear that was on the marble island. It fell to the floor, shattering into little porcelain pieces.

She had picked a simple sundress to wear, but was barefoot, and when he saw that she was about to turn and run again, and therefore step all over the shards beneath her, he moved swiftly. He had her up, in his arms seconds later, and set her on the counter away from the broken shards. The sound of crunching under his shoes was loud, but not nearly as loud as the sound of her frantic breathing.

He took a step forward, parting her thighs even farther. He placed both hands on the counter and leaned in until there was only an inch separating their mouths. "The sooner you realize that you're mine, Ruby, the easier this will be." He lowered his eyes to her chest, saw her breasts rise and fall violently over the top of her dress, and looked back at her face. "I like the fight in you and love the chase as much as I get hard from the capture." A small noise left her.

"You're terrified right now, but I bet if I slipped my hand under your dress your pussy would be wet." She parted her lips but didn't say anything. "You can act like you're frightened, and even *be* scared to death of me. That would be the smart reaction." He moved his hand to her dress, slipped the material up her thigh, and moved his fingers down her inner leg. He felt the heat from her cunt instantly. Pulling her leg even farther out, he touched her pussy lips lightly, spread his fingers through her slit, and grinned. "Fighting me only turns me on more, and gauging by how fucking wet your cunt is, it has the same twisted reaction in you, too."

This is insane. *You are insane.*

Ruby couldn't help thinking that over and over in her head, disgusted with herself and this man, because not only did she fear him, but she wanted him, too. He was such a beautiful devil, tempting her darkest desires, the ones she had only dreamt about and had never contemplated or spoken of for fear of ridicule and shame. She was his prisoner, his captive, and he was making it sound like she wanted this just as much as he did. This was just a physical reaction to his touch, right?

God, you are just as sick as he is. Here she was, perched on this counter after she tried to escape him, and he was saying these God-awful things to her, touching her like he had a right to, and she was doing nothing but letting him. All of these things made her humiliatingly aroused. She didn't want to desire him, didn't want his hands on her, but she was wet, just like he had said she would be. Damn him and damn herself for her misplaced desires.

She had to be demented. In fact, she knew she was. Who wanted pain with pleasure? Who dreamt about what it would feel like to be restrained? And who in the hell was wet and aroused when her captor chased her, touched her, and said filthy things to her? She should have slapped his face, made him hurt as much as she was inside, but she was too afraid of what he might do.

Ruby tried not to want these things, but she had told herself that burying her fucked-up wants would make them go away. She had thought that, at least. Ruby had hidden how she felt, moved on with her life, and blamed it on the fact she just wasn't normal, hadn't lived in a normal environment, and had a mother that had been cruel to her. Here she was now, wanting to claw Gavin's face, wanting to scream for someone to help her, but was also transfixed by the light blue of his eyes, and how he looked at her as if she was wanted.

He was warped and had this delusion that she was actually his. Ruby didn't care how much he paid for her and didn't care that she desired him. "Get the hell off me." Of course, he ignored her, and continued to rub his fingers through her wet cleft, making her want more and hate herself more because of it.

"You're so pretty, so soft and warm, so wet and mine." It was as if he was talking to himself for how low he spoke. He removed his hand from between her legs and she sagged in relief, but he didn't move away. He slid his hand up her arm, over her bare shoulder, and wrapped his fingers around the column of her neck. He wasn't applying pressure, but the heavy weight of his palm let her know that he could hurt her at any second.

She opened her mouth to scream, because there had to be someone else in this house, but his deep chuckle stopped her. "Scream, pretty girl. Scream as loud as you can." He leaned in until she felt his lips along her jaw. She squeezed her eyes shut because she didn't want to like the way it felt when he moved his mouth along her neck, or stroked her skin with his tongue. He moved his mouth to her ear and whispered, "It is just you and me here tonight, Princess, but if you want to be loud, I certainly won't stop you." He leaned back until he was looking at her. "In fact, I want you to make a lot of noise."

Then his mouth on hers and his tongue speared between her lips. When he pressed his tongue against hers, he groaned and tightened his hold on her neck. He tasted sweet from the wine, and the in-and-out action he was doing reminded her of something far filthier. "You will obey everything I say," he murmured against her mouth. "You will never deny me, never talk back." He spoke between nips and licks. "If you're a good girl, I will never punish you out of anger." He moved his thumb along the pulse right below her ear. "And if you're a good girl, I will give you whatever your heart desires, pain included." A gasp left her when he sucked in her bottom lip and moved his teeth along the flesh.

Ruby flattened her hands on his chest and pushed. She didn't want this, despite the wetness between her legs that coated her inner thighs, despite the fact that her heart was racing and it didn't have anything to do with the chase. But he was strong, God he was so strong. He growled and reached out far too quickly for her to comprehend, wrapped his hand around both of her wrists, and yanked her off the counter. Seconds later, he had her turned around. Hand on the center of her back, he pushed her forward until her belly was flat against the cold, hard, and unforgiving granite. Everything was happening so fast.

"Please, please don't do this." Begging probably only made him more excited, a fact he affirmed when he ground his erection, which felt huge, against her ass.

He didn't answer, just placed his hands on either side of her outer thighs, and slowly moved them up. Kneeling behind her, he gripped the bottom of her dress with his hands and the warm, humid feeling of his breath through the material, along with the feeling of his forehead resting against her lower back sent an array of emotions coursing through her. When the chilled air moved along her exposed bottom, her tears started falling harder and her breath came in harsh pants, moistening the dark counter beneath her head. However, all he did was groan against her as if he liked the fact she was terrified of him.

"I can smell you, Ruby." His words were low and deep, and she squeezed her eyes shut. "Your arousal coating my fingers makes my dick throb to be buried inside of you. You are so wet, Princess, so fucking wet for *me*." She struggled again, but he added pressure to her lower back with his hand, and growled low in his throat like some kind of feral animal. "You'd do well to remain still. I am trying very hard not to take you against the counter like some kind of fucking savage. I know this is your first time, but I will fuck you right here if you keep struggling and tempting me." That had her stilling and everything inside of her grew frigid. "You're a virgin and I don't want to cause any unjust pain, at least not the kind that you couldn't climax from." She held her breath and looked around frantically. The wickedness of his words and this situation had her on the verge of passing out. "Good girl."

He moved his lips over the top of her ass and took hold of each of her cheeks in his big hands. When he spread them and the cool air moved along the crease of her bottom she sobbed harder. He groaned, and she didn't have to look over her shoulder at him to know he was staring at the area he had exposed.

"You're so fucking wet for me." He speared a finger through her slit and she struggled, but he brought his hand down on her ass cheek so hard that she screamed out from the pain. "You fight me, but your body craves this as much as I do." He rubbed her between her legs again. "See, you got even wetter from that pain. You hate this, but you fucking love it." At the first touch of his tongue on her pussy, she cried out and tried to straighten up, but he gripped her waist in a bruising hold and pushed her up the counter until the tips of her toes barely touched the floor. And that was when he feasted on her like he was starving. He licked up the center of her, dug his fingers into her flesh until she cried out from the pain before sobbing harder because pleasure followed soon after. He was making her feel good, and she didn't want that.

"Please stop. *Please.*" He groaned against her soaked flesh and sparks of pleasure cascaded inside of her. "Oh, God." She flattened her hands on the counter, and when she tried to move away from his wickedly abusive mouth, all she ended up doing was push her ass in the air more and causing her pussy to grind more firmly into his mouth. His hold on her was painful, but what he was doing with his mouth between her legs felt so good. She hated herself at that moment for being so weak and for actually enjoying this.

He moved his head and sucked her clit into the hot, wet depths of his mouth, and that was the end of it. The depraved side of her came for this man, this evil monster that was using her for his own sick pleasures, and she was folding right into his embrace. He sucked even harder, and her breath hitched, but he wasn't done with her. She knew that with her very soul.

"Tonight is about pleasing *you*, Ruby. I'll make you crave my touch, my mouth, and eventually my cock. You'll look upon me as the only one that can ease your dark need." He ran his teeth along her labia and a gasp left her at the sensitivity of it. "And you do have a dark need, the same as I do. You are perfect for me, Princess." This had her kicking her legs out, but he easily twisted her on the counter until she was now flat on her back. He had both of her wrists in one of his hands, thrust above her head. "You will scream my name for more, cry harder when I give it to you, and you'll look at me as the only man that can give you pleasure from the pain." He murmured against her flesh, but was relentless as rubbed her clit.

"You're a sick bastard." She tried to block the ecstasy he caused inside of her, but he must have sensed that because he made a very low, dangerous sound and moved his other hand to the opening of her pussy.

"Sweet Ruby, your reluctance only makes me want you more, and that is saying something monumental since I want you very fucking badly as it is." He moved that thick digit around her opening, not penetrating her, but promising that he could take her right then with little effort. "You have me craving more of your delicious denial." He started to penetrate her with his finger. His shoulders and hand kept her pinned down, and his mouth and finger made her a slave to his desires. He was relentless as he flicked his tongue back and forth over her clit, but he only pressed his finger into her partially.

"You like that I'm a sick bastard because I can feel you getting wetter." The sound of his voice made vibrations on her clit and she bit her lip. Why did she have to be aroused? Why did his forcefulness and demands make her body feel like a fire had been lit from the inside out? It was wrong on every level and Ruby hated herself for her reaction. She wanted nothing more than to curl up in a ball and cry out her frustration and anger, but the wickedly depraved things he did to her had her craving more.

"I don't want this." The saltiness of her tears slipped into the corner of her mouth as the pleasure built inside of her with every press of his finger and flick of his tongue. He hummed against her and sucked especially hard on the little nub until she came for a second time. Gavin was relentless in his onslaught, and she knew he groaned not only at her surrender, but at the fact she had tried to fight him and failed. She didn't need to hear him say he enjoyed the pain, denial, and everything else that was so very wrong to reach his own desires. Her body betrayed her, and she felt nauseous from the pleasure he had given her. She had only been in his presence for a day's time and already she had failed miserably. Coming twice had her covering her face with her hands and crying silently.

"Shhh, sweet Ruby." He had her in his arms seconds later, and just held her. The soft, almost affectionate stroking of his hand down the back of her head was soothing as much as it was disgusting. She didn't want to feel anything but hatred for this monster, didn't want to press her face to his chest and breathe in the dark, spicy scent of the cologne he wore. And she especially didn't want to feel safe and sated in his arms because none of this was right or sane.

However, she didn't push him away, didn't try to run again. Instead, she let him carry her away. His physical strength scared her; the fact he could look at her and he could see right into her soul petrified her. She knew this with every part of herself, and vowed that she would try to escape. If she was going to be this man's sex slave, then she was not going to make it easy for him. On the heels of that thought, she felt even sicker because hadn't she just submit to him far easier than a captive should?

Chapter Six

Ruby listened to the deep, even breathing of Gavin beside her. After he carried her out of the kitchen, she had thought he would take her to the blue and silver room he had taken her to when she first arrived. Instead, he had taken her to the room across from that one. Presumably, it was his, and the dark-colored theme seemed to fit his personality well. It also made sense that he would want her in the room closest to his, but then she wondered why give her a separate room anyway if he meant for her to be his little plaything.

None of that really mattered when the end result was still the same. She had been lying on her back, staring at the white textured ceiling for hours. She was naked, as was Gavin; she hadn't fought him when he removed her dress, nor had she given any reaction when he got naked. Although she had tried not to look at him while he undressed, it was hard not to. His body was perfect with broad shoulders, thick biceps, and a well-defined chest, as if he worked out hard to get that desired effect. She was angry with herself for thinking such things, and for taking an interest in him at all, but it was hard not to when he was right in front of her and seemed totally unselfconscious with his nudity around her.

She glanced over at him. He was on his back with the black sheet draped across his waist. His abdomen showed the hard lines and ridges of his muscles, but the raised part of his anatomy below the sheet drew her eyes. He had been so very hard when he took his pants off, but all he had done was climb into bed beside her, wrapped his arm around her waist, and pulled her in close.

Then he leaned close to her and kissed her temple as if they were lovers. He had spoken to her for a few moments, telling her he didn't have to be back at work until the day after next, and would show her around the property. Ruby hadn't said anything and didn't care about his life in the least.

The bizarre and misplaced pillow talk had gone on far longer than she would have liked. She didn't want to associate with him, didn't want to find common ground. He just wanted her to be okay with all of this, to accept that this was her fate. Fuck that.

Now that he was finally in a deep sleep and she was no longer trapped under the heavy, muscular cage of his arm over her belly, she gathered her courage to move. Forcing herself to stay awake even though she was exhausted was hard, but escaping and the thought of her freedom were a very good incentive.

He had one arm over his eyes, and she knew if she was going to do this it had to be now. He had said they were in Europe, yet he hadn't specified what country. He said there were servants, but she hadn't seen any, and if he made it a point to tell her they would assist her with what she needed, Ruby had to assume they knew of his little buying women hobby, and were just as depraved as he was. That or they were complete morons.

Ruby pushed the sheet off her body and very slowly moved off the bed. Gavin stirred slightly, but his breathing was still deep and even. She stilled, though, waiting to make sure he stayed asleep, and when she was confident he was, she moved until she sat on the edge of the bed. The wood floor was frigid on her bare feet. Pushing off the bed and standing, she slowly made her way toward the dress that Gavin had taken off her earlier and draped over one of the fancy chairs in the corner. She kept her eyes on him as she slipped it on. Ruby wasn't about to go outside without any shoes, but aside from the stilettos and a few ballet flats she had nothing else. Walking over to an armoire as silently as she could, she grimaced and stopped when a floorboard creaked beneath her weight. Her heart was pounding a mile a minute, and her palms were clammy. She watched Gavin, expecting him to wake at any moment, but he continued to sleep. She breathed out, feeling relief, but far from feeling free just yet.

Inside the armoire were rows f his shoes, but also shoes in her size. After she grabbed a pair of designer flats that looked like she might be able to move quickly and not break her neck, she walked over to the door, grabbed the handle, and twisted it. Thank God, it opened silently. She pulled the heavy wooden door open just wide enough for her to slip through and then closed it once more. The sound of the grandfather clock in the foyer ticked down the seconds, but as if a warning bell had gone off, it chimed as it struck midnight. Ruby didn't know if it would wake Gavin, but she wasn't about to find out. She tore off down the hallway, the thick, oriental-style runner beneath her feet making her footsteps soundless. Gripping the banister of the stairs, she took them two at a time; when she reached the last one, she tripped over her feet and fell to the hard marble landing. A hiss escaped her as pain exploded in her kneecaps, but she pushed the discomfort away and scrambled up. The massive double doors that promised her escape were only a few feet away, and she limped over to them. Taking hold of the cold, brass handle with one hand and unlocking the three separate locks with her other, she pulled the heavy door open. A gust of wind whipped by her and moved her hair in front of her face, momentarily blocking her vision. The sound of the door upstairs opening and slamming against the wall and Gavin's hard, heavy footsteps coming after her had her already erratic fear increasing tenfold.

She ran down the stone steps, but all that was in front of her was flat, manicured lawn. He would surely see her, especially with the moon full and shining a silvery glow that illuminated everything. She only thought about that for a second before taking off to the left, where there was a forest made up of thin, willowy trees. The trunks were thin, unable to offer much in terms of hiding spots, but it was certainly better than the grassy land that was her only other option. She ran as fast and hard as she could, and although she shouldn't have looked over her shoulder, she needed to see where he was.

He was moving quickly toward her, still a good distance away, and if she didn't focus and pick up her pace, he would catch her. Her shoes were horrible for running, and with the thick vegetation below her, the almost spidery branches from the trees acting as arms trying to keep her prisoner, Ruby wasn't gaining as much ground as she would have liked. With all the crying she had done since being taken, she was surprised she had any left. They came, fast, hard, and salty hot. Her vision blurred, and her breath came out of her in hard, frantic pants. All she could think about was escape, and finding someone that might be able to help her. She had to have hope that there was something out there for her, and that there was someone that could empathize with her and save her life.

The sound of his feet crunching right behind her had Ruby moving faster, but she tripped over the tangle of fallen branches, losing one of her shoes in the process. She glanced over her shoulder again, and screamed when she saw how close he was. He wore only his suit pants, and although his feet were bare, as was his chest, he was moving swiftly toward her with a dark, determined expression on his face. He was mad, livid, and she could feel those emotions coming from him like a whip along her tender flesh. Despite her fear, and the horrifying images of what he would do when he caught her, a warm gush of moisture left her pussy. She felt disgusted at that fact, humiliated even. That had her screaming out and crying harder. This was a race for her life and sanity, a time when arousal should have been the furthest thing from her mind, yet his chasing her was turning her on.

She stumbled forward again and lost her other shoe, but she pressed on. Her feet hurt something fierce since she no longer had the protection of her shoes, and her arms burned from the thin, almost razor-sharp branches that surrounded her. But for as fast and hard as she was trying to escape, she knew she wouldn't.

She felt the presence of his big body right behind her and swore she felt the heat of his breath on the nape of her neck. Ruby screamed and kicked out when he wrapped an arm around her middle and hauled her right off her feet. She thrashed and cursed, trying in vain to get out of his ironclad hold, but it was no use.

"Calm down, Ruby. All you're doing is tiring yourself out." The rage in his voice was barely suppressed, and she shook harder.

"Fuck you." She thrashed some more. "Fuck you and your sick, demented mind." He had his other arm around her chest and she lowered her head and sunk her teeth into his forearm. He cursed and gripped her chin in a painful hold.

"You're a young lady, and should watch your fucking mouth."

He turned her around and stared at her with eyes that looked so damn frightening she closed her mouth and felt her eyes widen. He let go of her chin, lifted her up, and had her thrown over his shoulder in a matter of seconds.

"You're sick, you bastard." Ruby pounded on his back and kicked at his chest. He suddenly stopped, and the jarring motion had her stopping as well, surprise and fear filling her. Keeping her over his shoulder, he lifted her dress over her ass. A gasp left her as the wind picked up causing goose bumps on her exposed flesh. Before she could scream or struggle, he brought his palm down on her bare ass. A soundless cry left her at the sting he inflicted since it had not been a gentle spank. It had been full of force, full of his anger, and clearly punishment for her running. He brought his palm down once more, this time just as hard as the last one. She didn't hold in her scream this time.

"You'll be calm, or I'll have no fucking problem with throwing you on the ground right here and taking your virginity in the dirt like some kind of animal." He didn't say anything else for several seconds, and she knew it was because he really wanted her to think about what he had just said. Although she had seen him lose his temper earlier, he had spoken now in such a calm and collected manner—despite the profanity—that it was far scarier this time. "Do you understand me, Princess?"

Ruby couldn't talk, couldn't even breathe as her flesh grew red hot from his palm and the tingling between her thighs became almost too much to handle, but she nodded because she didn't want to be hit again. Realizing he couldn't see her nod, she offered him a small, quiet yes.

"I can be good to you, Ruby, or I can show you exactly what it means to really fear me. Because what I have shown you right now is nothing. The choice is yours on how I treat you and how I react." He was striding forward again, but she didn't fight it, and hung there like a rag doll about to be tossed into the flames of hell.

Gavin's blood pumped quickly through his veins. He was hot from anger and aroused from chasing Ruby through the woods. He strode into his room, kicked the door shut with his foot so hard that when it slammed the pictures on the walls shook from the force. Ruby had stopped her struggles, but her body was tense against his. He tossed her on the bed and she bounced twice on the mattress before scrambling backward. She was now pressed against the headboard, staring at him, a blush covering her cheeks, and a light sheen of perspiration on her face from her attempt to escape him.

She was scared, no doubt about that, but he also knew she was aroused. He had smelled her arousal as he walked out of the woods. Her ass had been right by his face, her cunt just inches from his mouth. It had taken a lot of self-control for him not to deliver on the threat of throwing her to the dirty ground in the woods and fucking the shit out of her.

For several seconds all he did was stare at her. There were several filthy things he wanted to do to her running through his mind. Of course, he had expected her to run, had anticipated it. He had been hard just thinking about it, waiting for her to run so he could chase her. His cock throbbed behind the fly of his pants, and adrenalin and endorphins were steadily filling every part of his body. He had meant to wait before he took her, to be gentle with her for the first time. He could be brutal, but he wouldn't be cruel. She was already high on fear, especially of him, but after her little escape attempt, he needed to show her that he was the one in control.

"W-What do you plan on doing to me?" Her voice wavered, and although her body trembled, she no longer cried.

"A lot of things, darling." She glanced around the room frantically. "Don't worry, Ruby, I won't do anything to you that you won't ultimately enjoy." She was already shaking her head before he finished. "But I shouldn't allow you to get any kind of pleasure for disobeying me." He took a step toward the bed. "Although I do so love to see you come undone."

"I won't enjoy anything you give me."

He chuckled softly and let his eyes move along her barely covered body. The branches had torn parts of her dress, and since she wore no undergarments beneath it, flashes of her peach-colored skin greeted him.

"So those two orgasms I gave you in the kitchen were you not enjoying what I have to give?" He walked over to his closet and opened it. He heard her shifting on the bed and looked over at her. "I suggest you sit right there, Ruby." He kept his voice low.

"Okay," she whispered that one word. He nodded and turned back toward his closet. The light clicked on automatically as he stepped inside. He instantly let his gaze land on the dark box sitting on the top shelf. He walked over to it, snatching it off the shelf. The weight was heavy in his hands, and his balls drew up tight at the thought of the items inside.

As soon as he had purchased her, he had made the call to procure the specific items in the box he now held. Adelbert and Drika, the two servants that ran the estate, were out for the evening, which was perfect because he wanted a still and silent house when he made Ruby scream.

He turned back toward her, saw her eyeing the box, and moved until he stood right beside the bed. "When I saw you on that stage, I immediately thought how lovely you would look in pearls." She knitted her brows, clearly confused by what he meant, but she would understand soon enough. "Take the dress off, Ruby." She didn't obey right way, and his patience had long since run its course. "Now." Her eyes widened at the harsh way he said that word, but she did obey. "Good girl."

She sat up so she was on her knees, pulled the dress off, and instantly covered her breasts with one arm and placed a hand over her mound. He shook his head. "You don't cover yourself from me." He stared directly into her eyes and purred in approval when she dropped her arms back to her sides. Her breasts were large for her small body, with pink tipped nipples. He let his gaze travel down to her smooth, flat belly, flared hips, and a pussy covered with a trimmed thatch of dark hair. There was more hair there than he liked, but that was easy enough to take care of later.

"Please," she said softly. "I'm afraid of you."

He smiled. His cock surged forward, throbbing in time with his pulse. "You should be." He moved closer, and she scooted back, but stayed on the bed. He set the box down and opened the lid. Inside, there were several strands of pearls and a small one-strip leather whip. Gavin enjoyed certain aspects of BDSM that could be construed as hardcore. He took out the items and set them on the bed. Ruby eyed them with a wary expression. "Lie on your back and spread your legs." It took her a second to comply, but she did, albeit slowly. "I realize that I shouldn't have been so lenient with you." He glanced up at her. She was staring at the items on the bed, but she must have felt his stare because she looked up at him.

He picked up the strand of pearls that had been reinforced to his specifications. "I have to be gentle with you, because you are very fragile, even if you like to show your strength." He ran the pads of his fingers over the smooth, creamy roundness of the beads. "I had this specifically made for you, had it rushed to our home before we got here. I just know you're going to look gorgeous in them."

"You want me to wear a necklace?"

"Yes, Ruby, but not around your neck." He placed a knee on the bed and moved closer to her. Her breasts shook slightly as he moved on the bed, and his dick throbbed painfully.

"I don't understand." Ruby still had a flush on her cheeks, but it also spread down to her chest and covered the big mounds of her breasts. Without answering, Gavin took hold of her hands and lifted them above her head. He unclasped the strand of pearls, wrapped them around both of her wrists, and secured them to the slates of the headboard.

"Do you understand now, Ruby?" He leaned over her, making sure the pearls were secure enough that she couldn't get out of them, but that they didn't cut off circulation. "I had these made so I can restrain you and do whatever I wish to your body." He sat back and watched her struggle slightly, testing the strength of them. "They can't be broken, and will do nicely to keep you right where I want you." He ran his fingers over the line of her jaw, down her neck, and over her collarbones. He stopped right before he made contact with her breasts. She breathed out hard, and the action caused those gloriously plump mounds bounce.

Her nipples were hard and appeared to reach for his touch. His mouth watered for another taste, but he stopped right before he made contact with her smooth, quivering flesh. He was tormenting her as much as he was himself. What he wanted to do was bring his palm down on her skin, over and over again, until every part of her was a vibrant red from his erotic abuse. He wanted his handprints marking her body like a primal claiming and he wanted to hear her beg for more.

"Do you want me to suck one of these hard little nipples into my mouth, Princess?" When he spoke, his lips brushed along the taut peak, and although she didn't respond, he didn't miss the way she clenched her thighs together. Turning his head to the side and looking up at her, he was surprised to see the clear arousal on her face. He knew that she was probably having an internal debate: fight him with everything inside of her or give into her desires. Because she didn't answer him, he leaned back and didn't miss the very small noise that left her.

"This is sick, tying me up like this, trying to make me think that I want this." She strained against the pearls once more. "I won't, you know. I will never want this, or you." He cocked an eyebrow and turned to grab the strip of leather. Curling his hand around the handle, he tested the weight in his palm. This had also been custom made, with an ivory inlaid handle and butter-soft leather. Being wealthy had many advantages.

"This will make a beautiful sound hitting your flesh, and an even more attractive sight when the red lines appear." She screamed out for help, thrashed back and forth, and tried desperately to free herself. He watched her, when he sensed her start to grow weary, only then did he *tsk*. "It is only you and me here, darling." She kept her legs closed tightly, and he had a pretty good idea as to why. Gavin wrapped his hand around one of her thighs, feeling her muscles tense as she prepared herself for what he was about to do, but he paid no attention to her resistance. He wrenched her leg out and looked down at her pussy. She was wet, so wet that her arousal glistened on her inner thighs. "I knew you were the perfect one for me."

Gavin had to adjust himself between her thighs so he could force her legs to stay open. Sliding his hand up her inner leg, he ran a finger along the cleft of her pussy, gathering moisture at the tip and swirling it around the engorged bud of her clit. She arched her back, thrusting her breasts out as a strangled sound left her. "You like this." She shook her head and clenched her teeth, so he added more pressure as he rubbed the bundle of nerves back and forth. "Tell me how much you like this. Tell me it feels good." She was still shaking her head, but her eyes were closed, her mouth was now open as she made inarticulate sounds.

"Why are you doing this to me?" There was no heat behind her words, and it didn't even sound like a real question. "This is so wrong."

"No, darling, it isn't. It is so right, and that is why it feels so good." He rubbed her clit back and forth. Back and forth. "Quit fighting yourself and just enjoy it." She was now lifting her hips, seeking more of his touch, and this pleased him immensely.

"Please," she sobbed, but there were no tears. "Why are you doing this?" she asked again.

"Why am I doing this?" She slowly opened her eyes, licked those lips that were made to suck his dick, and nodded. "Because you are like me, Ruby. We are one and the same. What *I* need only you can give me, and what *you* need only I can give you." He set the strip of leather on the bed beside him and used his free hand to unbutton his pants and pull the zipper down. He wore no underwear and his dick sprang forth. He grabbed himself and stroked his cock from root to tip. "I get hard when you struggle, Ruby." Twisting his other hand so he was now rubbing her clit back and forth with his thumb, he slipped a finger into her pussy. "And you get wet fighting me, making me get forceful, and feeling the pain I can give you, because ultimately that is what gets you off."

He just held his finger there, letting her feel the weight of it at her opening, and let go of his shaft to pick up the whip. The strip of leather was only about a foot in length, but that was all he needed for what he had planned. Lifting it high, he brought it down across her belly. She arched even further and cried out. He had no doubt it hurt like hell, but her nipples grew harder, her blush darkened, and a gush of moisture covered his hand. He brought the leather down once more and watched in perverse pleasure as thin red lines appeared on her flesh. Over and over, he rained it down on her, rubbing her clit back and forth, and keeping his finger at the entrance of her pussy at the same time.

"Oh, God." Her eyes were big, and he knew she was going to come, but he wanted her acknowledgment that she was his. He eased his ministrations, and she made a tearless sob.

"Tell me you are mine and that this is what you want. Tell me that although you are afraid you also crave my touch." Her eyes were so big and blue, and the way she looked at him had power surging though his body. It was this desperate look; a very vulnerable look that had nothing to do with the fact her life was forever changed. It was a look that pleaded for more even if she couldn't say the words just yet. He added pressure again to her clit, but did it more slowly this time. "Tell me, Ruby, and I promise to treat you the way you deserve. I will cherish you, Princess, worship your body, and give you the kind of pleasure only people like us can enjoy." She would follow his rules. The rules kept them both safe and appeased his darker needs. He didn't want to hurt her for the sole purpose of making her obey. He wanted to hurt her with the purpose of getting her off from that pain.

"This is not the life I wanted." She whispered those words, and although it wasn't what he wanted to hear, he couldn't very well be angry with her for giving him the truth.

"Ruby, we can't control the life we are dealt. This world is about dominance and submission, of give and take, and of pleasure and pain." Keeping his hand on her pussy, he leaned forward and brushed his lips along hers. "Just tell me, darling, and I can make your suffering go away. I can make both of our suffering go away." She shook her head, but he felt her resistance leaving her.

"I just want to matter." Her words were heartbreakingly honest, but only she would know the true meaning behind them. He added pressure to her mouth, kissed her ferociously and with everything inside of him. "I don't want to be afraid, but I am." He kissed her again, ran his tongue along her lips, and groaned against her mouth. He moved his thumb over her clit harder and faster and slowly pumped his finger inside of her to the first knuckle. When he felt her tense once more, he sucked her bottom lip between his teeth, biting down at the same time she cried out from her orgasm. It went on for several seconds, and she ground her pussy against his hand. Yes, the surrender he had been looking for, but he wasn't nearly finished with her yet.

Chapter Seven

Ruby looked up at Gavin as he positioned himself between her thighs. He had set the leather strip aside, and she couldn't help but look at it, feeling arousal and shame over the fact she had derived so much pleasure from the delicious punishment he had given her. It shouldn't have felt so right, but God it did. With her hands still bound in the pearls, she was at his mercy. A part of her that wanted to scream and lash out, but there was another part of her—this one far louder—that just wanted to stop fighting, stop resisting, and take what he had to give her. Ruby didn't try to stop him when he grabbed her inner thighs and wrenched them open. He dug his fingers into her flesh, and she knew there would be more bruises added to the ones that covered her hips from his earlier ministrations. With her legs pulled all the way apart, her muscles straining from the force, all Gavin did for several seconds was stare at her pussy.

"I'm going to shave all the hair from your pretty cunt, Ruby." He flicked his eyes up to hers, and then looked down between her thighs again. "I want what's mine completely bared, smooth, and lush so when I lick you nice and slow and then fuck you fast and hard, all you feel is *me*." It was hard trying to get enough oxygen into her lungs as she listened to his words. "But that is for another time."

He slipped his hands up her inner thighs until he framed her pussy. His thumbs were right by her opening, and the gentle back and forth motion of him moving those digits along her hole had a gush of wetness leaving her. Gavin pulled her labia apart and the cool air moved along her inner flesh. A moan left her and she tried to close her legs. Gavin's gaze was so penetrating, so encompassing, that she felt as though his gaze alone touched her, consumed her.

He reached for the leather strip again and her heart started pounding so hard she thought it would burst right through her chest.

"Please." In all honesty, Ruby didn't know if she was begging him to stop, or to hit her again. Those dark desires she had always felt deep inside of her were right at the surface, not about to hide any longer when Gavin was able to deliver what she desperately needed. But she felt as though she was betraying herself, and all the women on the stage with her, by allowing this to happen and actually enjoying it. "I don't want to do this anymore." Oh, she did, but she couldn't just submit so easily on the first night of her captivity, right?

His chuckle was low and deep. "You act as though you have a choice in the matter." He brought the leather across her lower belly and she winced in pain. He moved closer to her pussy with every slap and sting of that strip on her flesh. On the heels of that pain was the intense heat of her blood rising to the surface and tingling with renewed desire.

Then he was bringing that leather down across her pussy, over and over again, until hot tears fell from the pleasure and pain. She had already been so sensitive there, but he was causing her to swell and heat further. The look in his eyes was so frightening in its intensity that she knew, as gentle he had acted at times, that was so much more to him than that. "I want to see you come again, Ruby." His chest rose and fell as if he was out of breath, but his voice was strong and even, and so very in control.

It was hard not to succumb to the whispered temptation of his acts. "It's not right." She didn't know if she was saying that to him or to herself, but it didn't matter because she couldn't stop the pleasure moving through her. Teeth gritted and beads of sweat lining her forehead, she lost that battle when he took one of her nipples between his thumb and forefinger and twisted the peak. Unbelievably hard pain filled her chest and speared her right down to her clit. Neck straining, eyes squeezed shut, and wetness coming of its own accord, Ruby was crying as she came for him.

"That's it, Princess. You need the pain I give you as much as I need to inflict it upon you." He didn't stop whipping her pussy with that strip, or tugging at her nipple until she grew overly sensitive and tried to close her legs. He let go of her breast and she opened her eyes, watching him toss the leather aside. He shifted only long enough to rid himself of his pants, and then he was between her thighs once more, guiding his shaft to her entrance. The thick, long length between his thighs was intimidating.

"No, you won't fit." Although she knew in reality he would, the idea of him shoving that into her had anxiety and anticipation thumping through her. He knew she was a virgin, but he didn't respond, just rubbed the big tip of his erection up and down the center of her. She groaned in pleasure when he bumped her clit. He pressed the crown to her entrance and pushed in slowly. The burning sensation of him stretching her had her curling her fingers into her palms until the sting of pain made her loosen her hold. When the tip of his shaft pressed through her opening, he placed both hands on the bed beside her head.

"You will never know how good you feel to me." She opened her eyes, not realizing she had closed them, and stared into his light blue ones. When he stopped, she knew that he had come up against her hymen. Her palms began to sweat, and she felt perspiration line the space between her breasts. He flicked his eyes to the area she had just been thinking about, and to her utter shock, dipped his head and ran his tongue along the valley. He then pressed his mouth to hers and stroked her tongue with his. She tasted the saltiness of what he had just licked off her. "There is no going back, Ruby." He pulled out of her slightly, and in once quick, measured thrust, he tore through her innocence and buried himself all the way inside her body.

The pain was like nothing she had felt thus far. It burned as if she was on fire, and moisture gathered in the corner of her eyes as she tried to stop herself from screaming out. She didn't want to give him the satisfaction of letting him know the pain he caused. However, when she stared into his eyes once more she contemplated if that really was the truth.

He pulled out slowly and pushed back in at the same pace. He did this repeatedly, always keeping the same speed until she knew if her hands hadn't been bound she would have been clutching at him, clawing at him, and trying to hold on as she went higher. But the near-softness that had taken over him suddenly morphed as he picked up his pace. Darkness fell over his face, clouding his eyes so they looked like a turbulent storm instead of a crystal-clear lake. The discomfort had diminished, and every time he thrust into her deep and hard, bumping her clit, and cursing out filthy things, her pleasure mounted.

Gavin started thrusting into her so forcefully that she was moving up and down on the mattress and hitting the headboard every time he pushed back into her. Ruby felt her orgasm climbing, felt like she was going to explode from the inside out, but Gavin slowed his pace, as if he knew she was about to climax, and a soft groan left her. He leaned back on his knees and smoothed his hands up her side and over her breasts. He pumped into her at an almost bored pace, squeezing her breasts as if memorizing them, and then glanced up at her. She was right on the precipice of orgasm, but she couldn't quite reach it. She wanted to scream at him, curse him, and beg him for more because he wasn't giving her what she wanted, but she felt conflicted. This man had bought her. She was his captive. That realization had her lips parting.

"You want more, Princess?" He never stopped moving in and out of her. "I want you to ask me for what you want." He wasn't asking her to tell him she wanted to come. No, he wanted her to say her darkest desires aloud. He moved one of his hands up and circled her throat. It was a loose hold, but there was so much promise in it. *Stop thinking like that. This man is a monster and wants to use you as his sex slave.* However, he was giving pleasure as much as he was taking it. Before she knew what she was doing, she spoke.

"I want more." Those three words were uttered low, but there was a triumphant look on his face after she said them. He applied pressure to her neck, slowly tightening his hand, restricting her oxygen. Picking up his speed now, he plowed into her and shoved his big dick in and out of her pussy until she felt his balls slap against her ass.

"That's it, Ruby. Give it to me. Give *yourself* to me." On the third thrust, she came long and hard, Gavin squeezing her throat at the same time her orgasm peaked. She could breathe, but barely, and crying out her pleasure was not possible. Stars danced in front of her eyes and blackness started to cloud her vision at the intensity of it all.

"Yes." She didn't know what she was agreeing to, but that lone word tumbled from her mouth on its own. Ruby was aware of him all but slamming his shaft into her, and the discomfort grew, but that pain also had her pleasure heightening, too. Then he was coming, and the groan that came from him was so very deep and masculine that she felt her entire body tingle from it.

Although it seemed impossible, Ruby swore his cock thickened even wider inside her, and she felt the hot, powerful jets of his cum bathe her insides. After several minutes of him surrendering to his pleasure, he collapsed on top of her. However, it was only seconds later before he rolled away and lay on his back, breathing heavily. The post-euphoric buzz slowly started to wane, and she realized that she had given herself freely to her captor, and that he hadn't even used a condom.

Ruby looked over at him, her fear once again renewing at the thought of diseases and pregnancy. "I'm not on the pill." She could barely hear herself over the thundering of her pulse in her ears. "And what about STDs?" Ruby was clean, but this man could be carrying all kinds of nasty things. That thought was enough to have bile rising in her throat. He sat up and leaned over her without responding. Once he had the pearls off her wrists, she rubbed her skin and looked over at him, expecting him to say something, anything, about what she had just said. When he was lying on his back once more, he breathed out heavily.

"I have no diseases, Ruby. I am tested regularly, and the last time was right before I went to the auctions. I hadn't been with a female since being tested. And I know you're clean, given the fact you were a virgin." She swallowed, but didn't look away from him. "And pregnancy isn't an issue since I've had a vasectomy." Okay, so that was at least comforting. He put his hands behind his head and stared at the ceiling.

"You never wanted children?" Why she asked or even cared was beyond her, but she was curious why a man, who as far as she knew, had no other children, would get an operation like that. But maybe he did have children and a wife somewhere else. No, she didn't want to think about that, because that would make this already fucked-up situation even worse. He glanced over at her as if surprised she asked. Heck, she was surprised, too. But he didn't say anything at first and went back to staring at the ceiling.

"I don't think bringing children into the life I lead is very wise." *You mean the kind of life where you buy women and keep them for your own sexual amusement?* A frown settled over his face and she wondered if she had said the words aloud. "Not taking into account that my profession requires me to be away for long stretches of time, and that at times I hardly have a moment to myself, I don't think that would be fair to a child." Wow, he'd almost seemed human there.

Suddenly, she grew chilled and reached down for the comforter. But Gavin placed a hand on her arm, stilling her. "I think we should go over the rest of my rules now, Ruby." Something flickered behind his eyes, *something* that had the hair on the back of her neck rising with awareness. He reached down, grabbed the comforter, and pulled it over them.

"Thank you." Maybe showing him gratitude and acting like she wouldn't fight anymore would go a long way in not angering him. Because although she wanted to leave, she also knew that the chances of that were very slim.

"You're welcome, darling." He leaned in and she forced herself to stay still as he kissed her on the forehead. "Your obedience pleases me. Now, about those rules." He leaned back, but pulled her toward his body so she was pressed against his muscular side. The position would be awkward if she didn't rest her head on his chest, so for the sake of comfort, she did just that. But deep down, Ruby admitted that being this close to someone that actually wanted her, and looked upon her like she was a precious treasure, did make her feel very good.

"I do enjoy the darker side of things—and we have discovered you do, too—but I don't want to go too far with you. I don't want to get angry and punish you because of that. I want to give you pain, yes, but I want to do that because you like it as well." She nodded slowly. "This is your home now, and you must realize that sooner rather than later. You are not to leave the property. If you want to walk around, then someone will go with you. Until you can be trusted, I can't allow you to wander around by yourself." He glanced down at her. "It's also safer. Do you understand me?" She nodded again.

"Safer from what?" He brushed a lock of her hair off her shoulder, but she didn't wince or move away.

"You're a young woman, and there are plenty of depraved men out there that would like to do filthy things to you." He said it seriously, with a touch of warning and anger in his voice. Did he mean it in a general sense, or did he have enemies out there?

"You mean men like you?"

He gripped her nape hard and forced her to look at him. "Yes, Ruby, men exactly like me."

Her heart started thundering at his words. "Maybe you should let me go then." Ruby should have kept her mouth shut, but how could he lay there and act like she was safer in here than out in the world? The things he had already done to her were depraved in nature, whether she enjoyed them or not. She reminded herself of the horrors that she had imagined: chained in a filthy cell, starved, beaten, and raped repeatedly. Gavin wasn't the worst monster that could have purchased her. In fact, he had given as much as he had taken.

Aren't you a monster, too, Ruby? You can't act innocent if you enjoyed the pain he gave you. He pushed her onto her belly before she was even finished with that thought. Using one of his knees to push her legs apart, he settled his nude weight on her. The air left her at his size, and his erection prodded at the crease of her ass. How could he even be hard again so quickly?

He pinned her wrists to her lower back. "You'll do well to watch your tongue, Princess." His warm breath teased her ear, and she closed her eyes at the arousal that started pounding through her at his hidden warning. "I could chain you up right now, mark up your body until you writhe for more, and cry out for me to let you come." He placed a hand on her hip. "But I won't let you come. I'll bring my palm down on your glorious ass until you can't stand it and your flesh is a vibrant red." He ground his rock-hard dick into her ass and her mouth dried at the feeling of that length pushing deeper into her ass crack.

"My handprints will look so lovely on your body, Ruby. So very lovely." He moved his hand up her side and rested it on the side of her breast. "It would be so very easy for me to go too far in my desire for you." He ran his tongue along her cheek. "And I desire you so fucking much, I could suffocate you with it." He had his mouth by her ear, and with every word, his lips brushed along the shell of it.

"Okay," she said that one word again, the only one she could form at the moment. He had successfully aroused and frightened her with those few sentences.

"Good girl." He moved off her, but gave her right butt cheek a light smack before getting off the bed. "Let's take care of your feet." As he left the bed, she looked over her shoulder and watched him walk into the master bathroom. It was hard to concentrate and hate the man when he looked like he did. As superficial as that sounded, he was built like one of those Greek gods she had learned about in school. The muscles of his back flexed, and his ass was so very firm. Ruby had never been one to care much about those parts of a man's body, but seeing Gavin in the nude had her pressing her thighs together. He disappeared behind the door and she rested her head on the pillow. He hadn't told her to turn around, and she didn't want to anger him after the little speech he had given her. It seemed ironic that she feared pain so much, but her deepest desires revolved around that specific fear. Then she had sampled it first-hand, and it had been terrifying and liberating all in the same breath.

It was a testament to how deeply her need went that she hadn't even realized that her feet hurt. Lifting her head and looking over her shoulder, she lifted a leg and stared at the sole of her foot. Scrapes littered the bottom of it, and as she looked at them, they started to throb. Gavin came back with a basin and set it on the bed when he was close enough. Inside she saw some medical supplies. "Are you a doctor?"

"No." He started cleaning off her feet with gauze and peroxide, applied some ointment on the cuts, and started wrapping them.

"Where did you learn how to do this?" It wasn't as if he was operating on her or anything, but his actions were precise and his concentration solid. It looked as though he had done this before. Had he taken care of someone else where he would have had to know how to mend people? Had he been abused and tended to his own wounds? That seemed like the most likely cause. Although Ruby had never before been physically abused, she had endured the emotional and verbal kind all through her life. She knew that trauma like that could be why she enjoyed pain and pleasure. Maybe the same thing had happened to Gavin?

For several moments, all he did was watch her, and she felt like the prey of a very big predator. "I can assume what you're thinking." He shifted his attention back to her feet, applied a strip of tape to the gauze he'd wrapped around them, and rose to his full, over-six-foot intimidating height. He sat on the bed and gestured for her to face him.

"I wasn't abused as a child, wasn't tormented by my peers, or tortured small animals." Ruby didn't say anything, but she didn't need to because he started talking again. "My life was spent more with the nannies and the servants my father had on staff." He reached out and took her hand. Holding it in his much larger one, he stared at it as he traced her fingers with his own. "I suppose neglect could be blamed for how I feel, and what I desire, but that would be a lie." He looked at her. "I have always felt these things. Pain with pleasure has always been what I have gone to when I have wanted to feel free. It is what I want, and what I need."

There was no emotion on his face, but since she had been with him, he had kept those locked down pretty tightly. "I could have any woman I wanted; that is not me being egotistical, just stating a fact. The women that I have had lack the honesty of their emotions." He pulled her in close, cupped her face with his hands, and just stayed like that.

"But how could you possibly know that I would like these kinds of things just from seeing me?"

"I didn't know until I saw your reaction to me." He had said he knew she was the one for him from the moment he saw her on that stage. But how could he see that she would enjoy this? "I just wanted you and was bound to make you mine. I saw the fight in you, and that darker part of me wanted you to do the same with me. I wanted you to fight against me; tempt me as no other could, because your emotions would be *real*. They wouldn't be because of the size of my bank account, or my social standing. They would be bone deep, naked in all their glory, and only for me."

His hold on both sides of her face reminded her of being possessed, of this man owning every part of her. It was strange to feel that way, but there was no doubt that the look in his eyes was proprietary. "Let's get some sleep, darling." He pulled her back onto the bed and covered them with the blanket. Gavin pulled her close so she was pressed against him, and Ruby was just too tired to fight anymore tonight. He had shown her a side of himself that startled her, made her think that maybe her life wouldn't be so bad here, but she told herself that no matter how beautiful something was on the outside, the inside was what counted, and she was still his captive.

Chapter Eight

Ruby sat at the table, a plate of breakfast food in front of her, and two older servants bustling around. Gavin was at the other end of the table, a paper on one side and a cup of coffee and two slices of toast on the other. It had been a few days since she had gotten to the estate, and it hadn't been as bad as she imagined. Gavin had taken her around the property; he'd shown her the grounds, the glorious flowers that lined one whole side of the house, and talked about the time when he was younger. She wasn't surprised to find out he was the CEO of his company, that it had been handed down from his father, or that he ruled it with an iron fist. She had come to learn very quickly what kind of man he was: the kind of man that always got what he wanted. The two servants, who seemed to be the only ones that ran this huge place, kept to themselves.

She looked at Gavin, but his attention was on the paper. The night before he had held her so gently, and she could have imagined that they were lovers with mutual affection for one another. But they weren't, and she needed to realize that it didn't matter how caring he appeared, he had a darkness inside of him that was downright frightening.

What do you have back at that trailer with your abusive bitch of a mom? What did you think you could have in Fort Hampton?

"Ruby, I have to fly into New York today, and might not be back until tomorrow evening." He folded the paper and picked up his coffee cup. He watched her over the rim of the dainty cup, and she felt naked once again. It was clear this was her reaction whenever she looked at him. "I meant to stay here longer so you and I could get better acquainted with each other, but unfortunately, this matter can't wait." He set the cup back on the table and turned to look at the older gentleman whom she knew was named Adelbert.

Gavin started speaking to him in a foreign language. The man nodded, glanced her way, and then looked back at Gavin in response. He then called the woman back into the dining room. She held a tray of fresh croissants, and after she set them on the table, the three of them started speaking. Drika, the woman, couldn't have been too old, maybe in her early forties, but she had a perpetually pinched expression whenever she looked Ruby's way.

Ruby felt even more out of place as she was the only one that didn't know what the hell was going on. Clearly, no one was going to fill her in on the discussion since the man and woman turned and went back into the kitchen. Gavin grabbed his linen napkin and wiped the corner of his mouth. "You should eat more, darling."

She hated that he called her those little endearments. "Darling" and "Princess" didn't make her feel like he cared for her, but more like the object she truly was. But angering him was not her intention. If she had to be here, for however long that was, she didn't want to have to constantly fear that he would be upset and resort to the levels of punishment he had threatened her with.

Nevertheless, he was leaving the country, and that gave her the perfect opportunity to leave. "And if you're thinking that you could escape while I'm gone, Adelbert and Drika will keep an eye on you. They may not know exactly why you are here, but they know you are very special to me, that you need to stay here for your own good."

Wait, his servants didn't know she was a prisoner? If they didn't speak English, telling them that she was wouldn't do any good, but she still had to try.

The two servants came back in and gathered the dishes. She had eaten half of the food but her appetite was almost non-existent, and she'd had forced herself to finish that much. When they went back into the kitchen, Gavin leaned back in his chair and stared at her.

"What?" She shifted in her seat. It had been a few days since he had taken her virginity. Ruby was still sore between her thighs from his insatiable appetite. The warm baths he ran for her and forced her to take after they had sex went a long way in easing her muscles and the soreness in her body. However, he had taken her slowly this morning and touched her as if she really was a fragile and breakable piece of porcelain. Ruby didn't know how to feel about that exactly, because it had been nice, and he'd made her feel so good. The build-up had been easy, rising slowly until it broke free from her and she was gasping from it. And then he had helped her bathe, checked her feet once more to make sure they were still healing well—which they were—and kissed her lightly on the lips. He was like Dr. Jekyll and Mr. Hyde, and her head spun from the shifts in his personality. Now here she was, aroused once more with her pussy tingling even after he had gotten her off already. Why could he look at her, not even say anything, and make her feel so liquid?

"I'm just imagining you naked." His grin slowly changed the hard contours of his face. He had picked out what she was wearing. The white satin blouse had tiny pearl buttons, and at her neck, she wore a strand of pearls as well, as if he wanted to coordinate her attire and accessories. The pewter-colored skirt was loose and very feminine with tiny white flowers on it. Almost modest, it hung below her knees. Ruby had felt like a doll as he laid out her clothes and told her to dress for him, and she had felt even more so when he came up behind her and started running his fingers through her hair while he whispered very filthy things to her. She was his little sexual doll, one he could groom, dress, and do with as he pleased. Why didn't that bother her as much as it should?

"Drika will help you with any personal needs. Adelbert will be here mainly for the house upkeep, but since he is the only one that speaks any English—albeit not very fluently—he will help you as well." Well, that answered her question about the English. She'd have to search the house, maybe find a phone or laptop that she could use to access the internet. She could send an email to the FBI, or someone that could actually help her. She felt him watching her, and she looked up, not realizing that she had been focusing on her glass of juice for so long.

"Okay." She seemed to use the word a lot, but what else was she supposed to say?

"Oh, and just so you aren't rummaging through the house on a wild goose chase, there is no landline on the estate, and I take my cell and other electronic devices with me when I leave."

Shit. "What if there's an emergency?" She didn't care if she could get in contact with him, but maybe she could gather some information on where she could go if she needed help.

"Adelbert will contact me, and I can be back here quite quickly." Great, he was leaving her with people she couldn't even communicate with, and had no means to reach out for help. He stood, smoothed his hands down his three-piece suit, and looked at her. "Come here, Ruby." She slowly stood and moved around the table. Glancing down at his pants, she saw that they were tented. How could he be this insatiable? He had just had sex with her hours before, and by the gleam in his eyes and the erection he was sporting, it was clear that wasn't really an issue.

God, she was sore between her thighs, and her unused muscles protested even the simple act of walking, but it seemed her body didn't care, because she was wet, and suddenly felt so hot. When she was in front of him, he wrapped his hand around her hip, curled his fingers into her body, and pulled her close. There was discomfort from the bruises he had already left on her flesh. The purple and blue fingerprint-sized marks shouldn't have made this flush spread throughout her body as she looked at them, but they did. A deep sickness filled her that her first thought when seeing them was they were his marks of ownership. He moved his hand up to her neck again; she had already decided that he enjoyed holding onto that particular part of her body. Maybe it made him feel powerful, as if he could restrain her so very easily.

Of course, that was the reason.

"What are you doing?" She blinked back the need to close her eyes when he leaned in close and she felt his breath brush her lips. He smelled faintly of the hazelnut from his coffee. But he didn't kiss her, just kept his mouth perilously close.

"I'm enjoying you while I can. It's going to be hard—*I'm* going to be hard—being away from you." He pulled her even closer so their chests were pressed together, and she felt his erection prodding at her belly.

"But you said you wouldn't be gone long, right?" She was trying to get a better idea of how much time she had to try to escape again.

"It might not take me very long at all, Ruby. In fact," he brushed his lips lightly across hers. "I might be back as soon as tonight." He moved both of his hands to her shoulders and pushed her back. She blinked rapidly to get rid of the haze that settled over her. Maybe she was suffering from Stockholm Syndrome? Maybe she was demented, even more so than she initially thought. What other logical explanation could there be for her need to be by him after only being in his presence for such a short time?

He didn't kiss her and instead exerted pressure on her shoulders until she was on her knees and looking up at him. Her mouth instantly went dry when he let go of her and pulled the zipper of his pants down. It was erotically sick the way he pulled his erection out through only the flap, not even bothering to undo the button. This felt cheap in every way, but that didn't stop her from getting turned on even more.

You are sick, girl, so very sick, and you're playing right into his hands and loving every minute of it.

"Go on, Ruby; suck my dick with that very pretty mouth of yours." He stroked his finger along her jawline, moved it over her chin, and brushed his thumb along her bottom lip. "You'll be just fine at it, perfect even." Leaning forward, she felt her throat constrict at his large size. She wasn't a prude intellectually, but physically she had next to no experience in this kind of thing. She had been fingered once, made out a few times, and had given a hand job, but those had been such quick episodes that they were hardly memorable.

"I've never done anything like this before." She licked her lips and watched as a drop of clear fluid dotted the tip of his erection.

"You have no idea how much it pleases me to know that you are untouched in every way." She certainly wasn't going to educate him on the reality of what she had done sexually. Let him think what he wanted.

"I don't want to disappoint you." God, did she just say that? Yes, she did, but she tried to reason that she was playing a part, pleasing him so he was happy and sated, just until she could leave this place.

"Only disobeying my orders could disappoint me, darling." He continued to stroke her lip, and then slipped his hand in her hair, grabbed a chunk of the heavy mass, and yanked her head back hard enough that she gasped in pain. But she also felt a gush of wetness slip from her. Pressing her thighs together did nothing but pinch her clit, causing a shock wave of pleasure to race through her. With no underwear on, her nipples poked through the thin-as-hell blouse and her arousal made her inner thighs uncomfortably wet. "I guide your actions. Now, suck my cock, Ruby." He pulled her head forward until the slick tip of his shaft moved along her lips. She opened and sucked the head inside.

"Yes, that's so very good, Princess. Now move your tongue around." She did as he said, and the salty flavor of his pre-cum bathed her tongue. "Lick the underside of my cock, Ruby. Stroke it as if you were using your hand."

Flattening her tongue and doing what he said required her to take in more of his length in, but he was far too thick and long for her to suck all of him inside. She licked the underside, swore she felt the vein there pulse with excitement, and couldn't stop the moan that came from her. It certainly wasn't a flavor that she would have thought would taste good, but God it did, and in that moment, she didn't think about how she'd come to be in his presence. All she wanted was to please him because for some fucked-up reason that pleased her as well.

Letting her mouth do the work, she started sucking him with fervor. Taking hold of the root of his dick with her hand, she stroked what she couldn't reach with her mouth.

"That's it. Suck me until I come down your throat." He still had his hand in her hair, and kept her head stationary as he moved in and out, fucking her mouth like he'd fucked her pussy just this morning. Aside from the deep breaths coming from him, he didn't make any noises. Looking up at him, she saw his attention on her mouth. "You should see your lips right now, stretched wide around my fucking dick. It's such a damn turn on." He increased his speed until the tip of his erection slammed against the back of her throat. Gagging from the forcefulness of it, her eyes watered and saliva dripped down her chin. Despite that, she grew wetter. "*Christ*, Ruby." He was always in such control of his emotions, so hard and stoic. For one second, just one, she saw the human that lay behind his coldness.

A deep groan left him then she felt the hard jets of his cum move down the back of her throat and tasted the saltiness of it as it coated the interior of her mouth. He kept her prisoner with his hold on her head, and she had no option but to swallow it all. Slowing his thrusting hips, she felt his cock start to grow soft. He took a step back, slipping from her mouth, and she felt a drop of wetness slide down her bottom lip. Reaching out with his thumb, he moved it along her lip, collecting that drop of cum. He pressed the pad of his thumb back to her mouth until she opened for him.

"Suck it clean, Ruby." Eyes half lidded, he kept his focus on her mouth as she suctioned her lips around the digit. She ran her tongue around the tip of it, licked, and sucked off the slick fluid, and didn't stop until he was pulling it away from her mouth. Taking her under the arms with his hands, he hauled her up and slanted his mouth on hers. Apparently, he didn't care that he had just come in her mouth because he thrust his tongue inside, swirled it around hers, and groaned. By the time he moved back she felt hot and sweaty, and so very turned on. "Don't be bad while I'm gone. I have a nice little reminder on how good you can be, Ruby. Don't make me have to come back here earlier than necessary." His expression was once again hard, and he spoke while tucking himself back in his pants, zipping it up, and straightening his suit until he looked like a collected businessman once more. Then he turned and strode away, and a moment later, she heard the door open and close.

Ruby rushed to the foyer and looked out the window beside the front door. Gavin got into another stretch black limo, and she knew he was going to the hangar and small private airstrip he owned. She was all alone, well, aside from the two servants he had watching her. Did she risk trying to escape, failing once again, and having to endure whatever wrath would surely come from Gavin as a result? Or did she stay here, earn his trust, and hope that one day, hopefully very soon, he would take her into one of the towns where she could get some help?

"You are okay?" The deep thick accent came from behind her and she turned around to see Adelbert. He had a pair of very big and sharp shears in his hand. He must have seen the fear on her face as she looked at them, but he started speaking again, and then shook his head as if realizing she didn't understand. "For flowers." He lifted the shears, opened and closed them until she heard the distinct "clip-clip," and nodded.

She didn't know if she should be polite or give this guy the finger. She could open the door and try for the woods. Surely, she could outrun him. Eyeing him up and down showed Ruby that although he looked like he was in his fifties or early sixties, he was also in phenomenal shape. In fact, he looked just as muscular and toned as Gavin. *Why did you think they were that old?* Her inner question didn't matter because she still had to decide what she planned to do. It shouldn't have been a difficult decision, but for some reason, it really was.

Drika came in, her words fast and angry as she spoke with the man. They argued for a few seconds, and finally the woman threw her hands in the air and made an exasperated noise. She turned toward Ruby, gave her a once-over, sighed, and shook her head before turning and leaving. The older man started chuckling and pointed to where the woman had left.

"My sister, she is crazy," he said, laughing. So, they were brother and sister, and she was clearly a lot meaner that he was. "You go see flowers with me?" His English was pretty broken, and with his thick accent it was hard to make out his words, but she picked up on it enough.

He tilted his head toward the back, and she glanced at the front door. "You have seen the flowers with Master Gavin, yes?" She slowly nodded and clasped her hands together so she didn't fidget. "Then let us go." He smiled, and it appeared warm and gentle. She smoothed her hands down her skirt and decided to go with him, because for all she knew, Gavin was watching, and waiting for her to make her move. She had time, and she needed to use it wisely.

When she started following him, he grinned, and slight wrinkles around his eyes and mouth became evident. He led them through the dining room and into the kitchen. On the other side of the kitchen, there was a set of double French doors.

They stepped into a conservatory. It was large, with floor to ceiling windows that let in the warm morning light. There was wicker furniture around the room along with fresh and colorful tulips. The windows showed the back property, all flat, grassy land, with tall, swaying grass, and a blue picturesque sky. Ruby could see Drika out by a clothesline, stark white sheets fluttering in the breeze. It seemed weird to see a clothesline in this opulent estate.

"It is good for the soul." She glanced at Adelbert, who had a smile on his face. He was pointing at the clothesline. "Sun and fresh air makes everything happier." He didn't wait for her to respond, just motioned for her to continue following him. He led her out of the sunroom, to the back of the house where she knew there was a sea of colorful flowers. Even though she had seen them before, she still stopped and took in the sight.

All her life asphalt, grime, cars, and smog had surrounded her. But here everything was fresh, clean, and so very open. There were no buildings blocking the sky, no cars with noxious smog. Gavin was right; this place was so isolated it appeared untouched by man. She shouldn't be gazing at the land as if she wasn't the captive of the gorgeous, sadistic man, but she was. They were out in the middle of nowhere, but the scenery was so beautiful, all Ruby could do was sigh and take it all in.

"It is very beautiful, yes?" Adelbert questioned.

She nodded, not looking away from the rainbow of colors in front of her.

"I must fix the trees." He pointed to the endless row of willowy trees that lined the other side of the property. "But you can pick flowers for dinner?" She assumed he meant as a centerpiece for the table at dinner, and not actually to eat. Turning to face him, she watched as he looked down at her with that same pleasant smile.

"You know why he has me here?" She didn't wait for him to answer. The questions just flowed from her as her emotions spiraled. "He has me captive, held against my will. He bought me at an auction, and I fear for my life." She wasn't sure if the last was the whole truth or not. She didn't know how far he would go in his need to possess her.

"You are hurt?" As far as she could tell, he wasn't being sarcastic or cruel in how he phrased the question. He honestly seemed interested in her answer. "The Master of the Estate has harmed you?" *Master of the Estate?* She smoothed her hand down her skirt, felt the tenderness of the bruises that Gavin had given her, and opened her mouth to tell him that yes, the Master of the Estate had harmed her, and she had the marks on her body to prove it. Why did she feel it wrong to think that and say it aloud? Yes, he had hurt her, but she had enjoyed it.

It shouldn't matter that she had derived pleasure from it. However, before she could say anything, Drika was striding toward them in hurried steps. She stopped in front of them and looked at Ruby. Once again, she started talking quickly to Adelbert, but her eyes stayed on Ruby. "My sister has to keep a strict schedule and says I am talking too much with you. She says Master Gavin will not be pleased if our work is not completed." He chuckled at his own words.

Ruby watched as Drika walked back to the estate.

"Come." Adelbert set the shears down and took Ruby's hand. "Master Gavin told me to make sure you are happy, to keep you company. He says you are frightened, that you might run because of that, yes?" It was hard to get past his deep, thick accent and broken English, but the longer she was in his presence the easier it was becoming. "We are all captives of ourselves, yes?" She stared at him, not hiding her confusion. Had he taken her earlier words that she was speaking rhetorically and not literally?

She was so stunned at first that she allowed him to pull her toward the field of flowers. When they reached the edge, she glanced around and watched as they moved in unison when the wind picked up. It was like a colorful wave.

"Yes, the wonder of God, the glory of creation. We should enjoy it and not run from it." He was looking at her now, but took a small step back and held his hand out toward the flowers. She stayed still for a second, but then got down on her haunches, closing her eyes, and inhaling deeply to allow herself this moment of peace. She had never smelled anything so wonderful before. She opened her eyes and looked up at Adelbert. He reached into the small utility belt he wore around his waist and removed a gleaming pair of scissors.

"You help me, and we will talk." For some reason, she wanted to talk to someone, wanted conversation where she could stay by these flowers and enjoy the sun on her face. She reached out and grabbed the scissors he held out. He gestured to the flowers, and she grabbed a vibrant yellow one, bringing the blades across the stem. "Master Gavin helped me and my sister many years ago." She glanced over at him, but his attention was on the flowers as he cut them with another pair of scissors. "The town I lived in is very far away." He cut the flowers and set them on the ground. "Drika and I, we lost everything because of a fire, not only our possessions, but our parents as well." Although he spoke evenly, she saw the twitch in his eyebrows when he said those words.

"I'm sorry."

He reached out and patted her on the shoulder. "It was long ago, and death, it is a part of life." He reached out, cut the stem of a pink flower, and placed it right over her ear. "Master Gavin wanted land to purchase. Even young he held power. He heard of our misfortune and offered us refuge." He cleared his throat, and she felt sorry for him even though he was loyal to the man that she should despise. "Without him I don't know where we would be. He is a good man. He could have left us there, with nothing. Our village was poor. There was no one to help us." He set his last flower on the ground and looked over at her.

"I'm very sorry, I am, but I don't think you understand what I meant—"

He shook his head, but kept his smile in place. "My English, it is not good, but I understand. You must understand me, too, yes?" She had no idea what he meant. "Look around." He gestured to the openness. "Master Gavin is a kind man. You must think with this," he reached out and placed his big hand right over her heart, "and not with this," and then he moved that hand up to her head. "Happiness is not always where you think it is. Fear can make you run from it. You must look deep to see what you really want." He took his hand away from her and his smile faded.

"We are given only one life in this world, and there is no wrong way to live and enjoy it." For some reason, that last phrase pierced something deep inside of her, and she had to look away from him as emotion clogged her throat. "We all have secrets, ones that we try to bury deep inside of ourselves, but no matter how much we want to erase them, they are always a part of us." Ruby turned and looked at him again. It was as if he was speaking about her, as if he *knew* her. "We should embrace it."

He stood, tapped her on the head as if she was an obedient child, and turned back toward the estate. She watched him and then looked at the field in front of her and then at the woods. Was it really so bad being here? It wasn't about the money that Gavin clearly had, or the possessions that surrounded him. This was a very beautiful home, and the land was breathtaking.

She had to ask herself if she wanted to leave the only person that actually made her feel something other than loneliness and despair. Sure, the way they met was less than conventional, and there were aspects of Gavin that frightened her, but when she was around him and he touched her, she felt *alive*.

Ruby stood, not sure, at that moment, if she would run or head back inside. Looking over at Adelbert, who now stood by the backdoor, she knew that strangely, she didn't want to run as badly as she had that morning.

"You bring the flowers, and I will show you how to make *Jodenkoeken*, a very delicious butter cookie." Ruby couldn't forget about how she had gotten here, or why she was still here, because it wasn't that easy. She just couldn't discount the fact that Gavin made her feel *alive*. She was more than just someone that took up space. She looked down at the flowers at her feet, bent to scoop them up, and rose.

She started walking back toward the estate. She knew that her life before had been a horror of its own. She had been a captive of her circumstances. Ruby wasn't so sure that going back out in the world was what she truly wanted. Adelbert's words re-played over in her head. They made so much sense, and it was as if he had been speaking to her soul.

Chapter Nine

Ruby stared at her reflection in the bathroom mirror. She was in the room Gavin had taken her to when she'd first arrived, even though she hadn't actually slept in it until tonight. She rested her hands on the counter, bent her head, and closed her eyes. She was very tired, but for over an hour, she had lain in the bed staring at the shadows moving across the ceiling.

The idea of staying in this mansion with Gavin scared her; the way he made her feel scared her. What frightened her more, however, was what lay out there in the real world. She'd never tried to pretend that she was perfect or lived a gilded life. She had survived solely because she had wanted to live. If she had left it up to her mother, she would have died a long time ago. Despite the fact that Ruby had never felt like she fit in, had always been an outcast in school, she had pressed on, because the alternative was not acceptable.

She lifted her head and looked at herself in the mirror again. Her dark hair was wet from the shower she had just taken and hung in loose waves around her naked body. Not able to sleep, she had thought a warm shower would help, but it hadn't relaxed her; it merely amplified the fact that she was tender, and that every part of her tingled with awareness.

If she closed her eyes, she could practically feel Gavin touching her. A shiver worked through her. Her skin looked pale under the bathroom lighting, and the bruises Gavin had given her stood out like a beacon. She straightened and ran her fingers around the fingerprint-sized ones on her hip, moved her hand down her thighs, and touched the ones that lined the flesh of her leg. Why did seeing those make her feel special and cared for when it should have made her feel abused and violated? *Because when he gave them to you, a dream sprang forward inside of you.*

She had never been loved, never felt wanted, not even with the few boys she had attempted to spend time with. They had only wanted one thing from her, and when she hadn't given it to them, they had discarded her just as easily as everyone else had.

She'd felt cared for when Gavin touched her. She'd seen the way he looked at her, like a treasured possession. There was a lot of evil in the world, and she had seen it firsthand. Can an act born of evil ever become something pure?

After she had picked flowers with Adelbert and carried them back inside, she knew she'd just made a monumental decision. She spent the remainder of the evening in the mansion with Adelbert and Drika. They didn't know that he enjoyed sadistic sexual play, nor did they know she was his masochist. To them, Gavin was their savior.

She ran her hand over the mirror once again when it started to fog up. "Well, what are you going to do?" Silence greeted her as she looked at her reflection. She turned and grabbed the plush robe that hung behind the door. After she put it, on she opened the door and turned off the light. She knew she wasn't alone as soon as she stepped into the room. It took her eyes just a moment to adjust to the darkness, but she saw him sitting on the edge of her bed, and felt his eyes on her.

"Hello, Ruby." Gavin's voice was deep, and now that her vision was clearer, she saw he wore a suit, but he wasn't as impeccably styled as he usually was. He wasn't wearing a tie, and the first few buttons of his shirt were undone. His jacket wasn't buttoned, and the vest underneath was visible.

"You're back." She didn't know why she was surprised to see him; he had said he might be back tonight. Was she disappointed that he was already home? That he hadn't stayed away longer? No. That realization had her heart racing and her mouth dry.

"Come here, Ruby." His voice was low, and even though he sounded exhausted, there was that ever-present assertiveness and dominance laced in his words. She stepped away from the bathroom and closer to him. She stopped in front of him and hated the fact that her breathing had increased just at the way he looked at her. The moon was full and the silvery light came through the window where the drapes were half closed. "Did you miss me?" He reached out and tugged on the belt that held the robe closed. She didn't stop him as he undid the knot, nor when he took each side of the robe and parted the material.

She was naked underneath, and a deep noise left him when he saw what she had done. "I see you did miss me." He ran his finger over her freshly shaved mound. Why had she shaved all of her pubic hair off? Honestly, she didn't know. "You must have thought about me a lot to have done this." He looked up at her, and even though exhaustion was evident around his eyes, he looked so damn good. Like a fallen angel.

Ruby had found herself in the shower, with a razor in hand, and thought how pleased Gavin would be if he saw her completely free of hair. He stared at her pussy for a long time, ran his finger along her now smooth, slick cleft, and groaned. Gavin pulled her closer. All he did was press his head to her chest, breathe her in, and hold onto her.

It was a very affectionate embrace, and Ruby found herself lifting her hands and spearing them in his hair. The thick strands weren't like his normal perfectly styled appearance. It looked like he had already been running his hands through it. He tensed momentarily, maybe just as surprised as she was at this intimate action. She couldn't explain her actions to him; she couldn't even explain them to herself.

"You left the razor. You must not have been too worried about me hurting myself." Ruby didn't know why she had even brought that up. Bringing it to his attention that she had actually thought about hurting herself—which, honestly, she had for a spilt second—might make him even stricter. He leaned back to look up at her.

"Did you want to hurt yourself, Princess?" His voice was soft, but she wasn't fooled. He lifted his hand and stroked his finger along her cheek. She thought about how to answer, but knew honesty was the only thing he would accept. He would know if she was lying anyway, that she knew without a doubt.

"I thought about it." The words were almost a whisper, and a flash of darkness washed over his face. In the next second, he had her on her back on the bed, with her hands pinned above her head and her thighs spread wide to accommodate his hips. He was hard, and his erection nudged at her bared opening. There was nothing stopping him from plunging inside except for the thin layer of his pants.

"Is your time here so horrible that you would resort to harming yourself?" He thrust against her and pleasure rocked her when he rubbed her clit. "Have I treated you so badly that you want the coward's way out?" He leaned down so they were nose to nose. "Have I not given you pleasure and seen to all of your needs?" He thrust his hips forward once more, nudging her clit and causing a moan to escape.

"And pain. You've caused me pain, too." He bared his teeth, and it was a frightening display of his anger.

"Yes, and you cried out for more and came undone. Right, Ruby?" He tightened his hold on her wrists until she opened her mouth and cried out silently. He kept pumping against her, right on her clit, causing her to become wetter. "I've said it once, and I'll say it again. You and I are the same." He let go of her wrists with one of his hands and moved it down to between her legs. He kept her in a secure hold with his other one, letting her know without words that he was the one in control. But Ruby knew he was in control. He made sure she never forgot that. Spreading her wetness around with a finger, there was a very satisfied look in his eyes.

"You can call it whatever you want, and deny it until you can't breathe, but the life you had back there doesn't give you the satisfaction that I do." He removed his hand from her pussy and pressed his finger into her mouth. "Suck it off, Ruby. Lick off the arousal that you got thinking of all the dirty things you want me to do to you."

"I hate you." There was no heat in her words, and he pressed his finger deeper into her mouth.

"Fucking lick it clean, Princess." She ran her tongue along his finger, tasted her flavor that coated him, and shouldn't have liked it as much as she did. He took his finger from between her lips and claimed her mouth with his own. Swirling his tongue along hers, his flavor mixed with hers until she was panting against him. "If you want pain, *I* will be the one to give it to you," he murmured against her mouth. He leaned back, and his hard expression spoke louder than anything he could have said. "Do you understand me, Ruby?" When she didn't respond quickly enough, he slammed his mouth on hers so forcefully that their teeth clashed together. "Fucking tell me you understand."

She nodded. "Yes. Yes, I understand." She might have thought about it, wondered what that kind of escape would bring, but she would never have done that to herself. She didn't say that, didn't tell him that she would never take her own life, no matter what. She wasn't strong enough to do that. He looked down at her once more, but showed no emotion. She expected him to fuck her right then, to make his point in a purely physical way, but he didn't. Instead, he moved away. She laid there, her legs still spread, her pussy and breasts on full display, and his hard-on still tenting the front of his pants.

"Get some sleep." He turned and headed toward the door, but before he left, he stopped and turned to look at her once more. "Every room in this estate is monitored. There wasn't one moment that I didn't know what you were doing, and if I thought you would have really hurt yourself someone would have been at your side in seconds flat." He opened the door. "And don't touch yourself. If you do you'll regret it." He left her lying on the bed, her heart thundering, and her body so aroused but with no relief in sight.

Gavin didn't go back to his room after he left Ruby on the bed looking deliciously submissive. He knew she would have given herself to him very easily, but his emotions were running high at the idea that she had actually thought—even for just a moment—about harming herself to get away from him. He headed down the stairs and into the kitchen. He needed a drink, needed something to help him unwind and ease the ache in his balls.

Staying in New York until tomorrow had been the plan, but he had gotten through all of his obligations with work and had taken the jet back to his estate. He was jet-lagged, exhausted, and horny as fuck. All he wanted to do was bury his dick inside of Ruby, and then when they were both sated, he would fall asleep, his body still connected with hers. But he had left her, and he knew that punishment would be far stronger than tying her up and bringing his hand across the luscious mounds of her perfect ass.

He pushed the kitchen door open and saw Adelbert. "It is late. You should be sleeping." He spoke to him in their native language, and Adelbert stopped and looked over at him.

"Master Gavin, I didn't even realize you had returned." Adelbert dried his hands on a rag. "I was in the cellar fixing a pipe that had busted. There was water everywhere."

"It's fixed now?"

Adelbert nodded. They stared at each other for a moment, and the other man turned and opened the liquor cabinet. He grabbed a bottle of thirty-year-old Scotch. The alcohol was nearly as old as Gavin. It had been his father's, one that he'd bought while away on one of his many business trips. Gavin didn't know why he had saved it. After his father died years ago he'd gotten rid of the majority of his belongings. The memories of the isolation and loneliness had come back every time he had looked at Warren Darris's possessions.

Adelbert didn't say anything as he grabbed two glasses and poured two fingers of the amber liquid into each of them. He handed Gavin a glass, and they both sipped on the smooth alcohol.

"Everything went well in New York?"

Gavin nodded. "It was quick, and I'm exhausted, but sleep isn't something that I think I can do right now." They sipped their Scotch in silence for several seconds. "Yeah. Darris Industries is now merged with Crowe & Barrett."

"Excellent. That is a reason to celebrate."

Gavin's business dealt with investments on a consumer and corporate level. Once the merger agreement was signed he had immediately come back, but *she* hadn't been far from his thoughts or his sight. Was he ashamed that he had watched her from his laptop on the plane? No, he needed to know where she was and what she was doing at all times. She was his, and not just because he'd bought her. Their time together had been short thus far, but he had no intention of letting her go. Had he thought she would try to escape as soon as he left? Yes, but she wouldn't have gotten far.

"Do you want to talk about it?"

Gavin tossed back the rest of the alcohol and gestured for more. Once his glass was filled, he took another sip. No, he didn't want to talk about it, but Adelbert was very good at reading others.

"Not particularly."

The look Adelbert gave Gavin told him that it wasn't an acceptable answer. "The girl is very frightened."

Gavin knew Adelbert was right concerning Ruby's fear. He saw it every time she looked at him, but beneath that she was aroused and curious about what was happening between them. In fact, he saw that she leaned into him when he touched her. Were they falling in love? No, it was far too soon for emotions like that. People like the two of them were a special breed. He had learned that a long time ago, accepted it, and now embraced it.

"Yes, I know." He tossed back the rest of his Scotch. Maybe he should have enjoyed it slowly, but right now he needed to feel something other than the need to go back up there and take her the way he wanted to. "She'll come to enjoy it here." Although Gavin hadn't known much about her at first, it hadn't been hard to get the information he needed. He had money, which meant he had connections everywhere. It had taken a little of time, but as soon as the agreement had been sealed, he had some of his associates gather what he needed. He had found out exactly who she was, where she had lived, and what she had been doing in Fort Hampton. She had led a life vastly different, but strangely similar, to his. Although he had not been abused, they had both led solitary lives, and both had wanted to escape at some time.

"I don't interfere in your personal affairs, but I think you need to speak to her and let her know that whatever reason you brought her here was to make sure she was safe." Gavin hadn't told the other man his reasons for bringing Ruby here, and there was no doubt Adelbert was curious about the truth. "I spoke with her outside, and I can tell you and she are cut from the same mold." He glanced at Adelbert. He knew about their conversation, and although there were cameras on the outer perimeter of the estate, and he had seen her looking so lovely amongst the flowers, he hadn't been able to hear what they were saying. But Adelbert had called him and told him everything, and he wasn't surprised that she had tried to reach out to his servants for help. "She says you harmed her, that she is a captive here."

Although Adelbert and Drika were the closest people he had in his life, it didn't mean he shared his darker desires with them. He hadn't told them he purchased her at a sex-ring auction. They did not question his asking them to watch over her, to make sure she didn't run off and hurt herself. They were loyal to him and did as he asked without complaint or suspicion because to them he had saved their lives. Gavin didn't think he was a savior in any sense. He had needed help at the estate as much as they had needed him. It had been a give and take companionship, and it had worked out well for years now.

But Adelbert was an old soul, could read people as if he'd walked in their shoes his whole life, and Gavin wasn't foolish enough to think that he hadn't picked up on something right away. In the past years when Gavin would bring women to the estate to try and sate his depraved needs, it hadn't taken the other man long to question him, especially when the women that left had marks on their bodies. But he was never judged, never condemned by Drika and her brother. Then Adelbert had wanted to know the reasons, and Gavin trusted him enough to divulge the sick, twisted needs that only certain acts could ease.

The women had always been willing. Until Ruby. But Gavin felt no remorse in buying her. If he hadn't... he didn't even want to think about what her fate would have been, where she might be, or who she would be with right now.

That might have been his first time at one of those auctions, but he knew the men that visited them. They were like him, but they were also different. They were cruel, had harems of females, slaves to do with as they pleased. Having her with him was much safer for her.

"If she is not here of her own free will, no matter the likeness you two share, you must rectify that."

Gavin set his now empty glass down and stared at the man. "And would you have helped her escape if you had known this truth in the beginning?"

The other man was silent for a few seconds and lifted his glass to finish off his drink. "It is not my place to interfere in the lives of others, especially the Master of the Estate, but I knew that something wasn't right with your relationship with the girl. This wasn't like the other times you had female company over." That hadn't answered Gavin's question, so he waited for Adelbert to continue. "But to answer your question, yes, I would have helped her if I had known she truly wanted a way out."

Gavin swallowed at the thought of Ruby out there alone. "I want her safe. I don't harm her, not in the sense you are thinking."

Adelbert nodded, but didn't respond. Gavin may have only had her for a few days, but the thought of her absent from his life was not something he wanted to dwell on.

"You must decide if you want a life where she has no choice, or if you want her to come to you willingly. Those two are vastly different, no matter how you try to twist them to fit together." Gavin didn't know how to respond to that. "I saw the way she looked at the flowers and watched how she reacted to my words. I might not have known she was not here of her own free will, but I knew she was a prisoner inside herself. She is a girl, lost in here." Adelbert placed his hand over his heart. Adelbert took both glasses to the sink and bid him good night, but Gavin stayed there for several minutes, thinking about their conversation.

He left the kitchen and headed back up the stairs. He pushed open the door to the room where Ruby slept and leaned against the frame, just watching her. She was curled in a ball in the center of the bed, still wearing the bathrobe, and her hair a dark mess splayed over the white pillow. Yes, he might like pain, might thrive on it and yearn for it, but that didn't mean he couldn't enjoy her softness, or be gentle and easy with her. Those moments might be few and far between, but they were there. Pulling the door shut and walking to his room, he contemplated showering and slipping into bed with her. Instead, he stayed in his own room and let his exhaustion take him under.

Chapter Ten

Two weeks had passed since Ruby arrived at Gavin's home. With each passing day, she found it harder to separate her need for freedom from her desire to be with him. He'd showed her two sides of himself and she couldn't help but gravitate toward them both. The angry, determined, and so-dominant side called out to the part of her she'd always tried to hide. She wanted what he had to give her even if it caused her to cry out in pain.

And then there were the times she saw this gentler side, the part of him that she sympathized with. It was like looking at herself, a lost and lonely soul that didn't want to be alone any longer. Had what he'd done been right?

At first, she had screamed and kicked out her response, wanted nothing but to escape and go back to her old life, but with each passing second, she knew that she didn't have an "old life." She had just been moving through each day, hoping that things would look up. Well, things had looked up. Gavin gave her the pleasure she craved, touched her the way she only dreamed about, and provided for her in a safe environment. There was no one looking for her, and she knew her mother wouldn't have gone out of her way and filed a missing person report. She was all alone, with only herself to look after, and no one that cared. Well, no one until Gavin.

With every lash of his hand and thrust of his hips, he showed her that there was no disgrace in what they enjoyed, and that they had found a special kind of desire with each other.

"What are you thinking of, Princess?"

She glanced over at Gavin. They were in the sunroom, she was sitting in one of the wicker chairs and Gavin in the one across from her. He had a newspaper in his lap and a coffee mug in his hand. He watched her expectantly, and there was genuine curiosity in his expression. "You're thinking of your home?" She sat up straighter. They hadn't talked much about her personal life, but it was mainly because she didn't want to, and thankfully he hadn't pressed.

"Yeah." She had to look away from him because his blue eyes saw too much. But it was hard to *not* look at him, too.

"Look at me, darling." When she had first arrived, she hated the endearments he used, but now she knew that it was his way of showing that he cared, that she was special to him, and that made her feel good inside. He was wearing a pair of navy slacks and a light blue sweater which brought out the color of his eyes. She was used to seeing him in his three-piece suits because that was what he mainly wore. "Tell me." She glanced down, but quickly looked back at his face.

"I was just thinking how differently my life has turned out." It was partially the truth. But when he leaned back in the chair and continued to stare at her, she knew that he wanted more. "It's just that no one is searching for me. No one cares that I am gone." She looked down at her lap, not caring if he got angry over it.

"I would care if you were gone." She snapped her eyes up to his, and warmth filled her.

"I wanted to leave here so badly, to go back home, but I don't have a home to go back to. My mother is a drugged-out alcoholic that did nothing for me except ignore me, try and drag me down with her and then use me for money." She looked back up at him, but he had a stoic expression, as if none of this was surprising. He either didn't care—which she knew was not the case—or he already knew all about her. "You know already?" Although she really shouldn't be that surprised, she still was.

As far as she guessed, the men who had taken her couldn't have known much about her, not if they targeted her from the motel. Most likely they had just spotted her, saw she was alone, and taken their chances. But Gavin knew her name, so it was idiotic to think that he wouldn't looked into her previous life. But still, for some unexplainable reason, it hurt that he was just now telling her. *But you didn't offer to tell him about yourself, Ruby. You can't be upset at him.*

"Come here, Ruby." His voice brokered no argument, but she didn't want to put up a fight. Ruby actually wanted to feel his arms around her, to know that she truly wasn't alone in this world. She stood and made her way over to him. He immediately reached for her and pulled her down on his lap. Gavin brushed her hair away from her face, then cupped her cheek. His hand was so big that it encompassed the entire side of her face, and she couldn't help but lean in.

"Yes, I know all about you." She didn't say anything, but she had known, given the way he reacted. "It was imperative that I know everything about you, Ruby." He leaned in and kissed her softly. This was the sweet and kind side of Gavin; she could look into his eyes and see that he was comfortable and at ease with his actions and ready to offer insight into his actions.

"Why didn't you tell me?" Ruby asked.

He placed a piece of hair behind her ear, and seemed to scan her face, almost as if he were searching for something.

"I know I haven't been very forthcoming with information," she admitted.

"No, you haven't." Gavin said and smiled at her. He pulled her closer to his chest. "But I needed to know about you for obvious reasons, and once I found out, I didn't feel there was a need for me to inform you. You are starting to acclimate well here and bringing up that I'd dug into your past wouldn't have changed the situation. Besides, I didn't feel that was imperative information for you to have, Princess." At first she hadn't felt anything but warmth at being in his arms, but after hearing all of that she couldn't help the outraged feeling inside of her.

"I understand why you looked me up, but you didn't think it was imperative information for me to know?" His smile faded, but he didn't respond. "I have started to feel connected to you, that you and I share something that no one else does." He opened his mouth to say something, but she continued talking. The look on his face told her that pissed him off. Well good, because she was pissed, too. She moved off his lap too quickly for him to react. His easygoing expression morphed to annoyance, and then anger when she started to back away. "You may have purchased me, but I thought you saw me as something other than a piece of property."

"Ruby, I suggest you calm down."

"I was calm until you made me feel unworthy." Maybe she'd finally let all of this built-up energy escape.

He stood quickly, and his face took on a frighteningly hard mask. "I have never fucking made you feel unworthy. In fact, I have always shown you that you are worthy." He was yelling now, and she shrank inside a bit. He advanced on her slowly. "You're acting like a child right now, Ruby."

She wiped away the angry tears that fell, hating that she couldn't control her emotions. "Maybe that's because I am a child, Gavin." He made a low sound, and a chill slid over her body.

"You sound ridiculous, Ruby. You're not a child, but you're sure as fuck acting like one." The warmed glass stopped her retreat. "Tell me exactly why you are so angry, and don't lie to me." He said the last part as if he were trying to stay calm, trying to make sure she didn't disobey him, but it didn't completely smooth out his rough exterior.

Honestly, she couldn't even answer that. She knew her reaction was ridiculous, but it was like something had snapped inside of her. In a move she hadn't anticipated, Gavin slammed his hands on either side of her head with so much force the glass shook.

He leaned in close and she smelled the Irish cream he had put in his morning coffee. His blue eyes flashed with his unrepressed anger. "Don't fucking make the mistake of thinking that I won't punish you for the way you are speaking to me. This little outburst will not go unpunished, and the fact you can't even tell me why you are upset pisses me off more."

In a gush of words she said, "Because my life was shit, Gavin—shit, and you went and dug around. I didn't tell you about it because I hated it, hated what it almost turned me into." She was breathing heavily now, her fear pounding through her veins like an erratic drum. Of course, her traitorous body grew pliant just being around him. He was huge and towered over her, and although he was furious with her, he was hard between his legs. His cock pressed right into her belly, reminding her that he might hate that she acted out, but he also loved it.

He gritted out, "You are embarrassed over your former life, and you thought the best way to discuss your feelings with me was to act like this?"

She swallowed down the nervousness in her throat. When he said it like that it sounded ridiculous, but she hadn't been able to control herself. It was like a dam had broken inside of her and there had been no stopping it. He didn't speak, but she watched his eyes take in every part of her face. He leaned back an inch.

He wanted her, just as much as she wanted him at this moment. Both of their emotions were high, his annoyance and anger, hers embarrassment and shame. She had been foolish to think that he would never know about her life with her mother. But she still hadn't answered him, and she knew that angered him even more.

He made another low, almost animalistic sound, and grabbed her upper arm. He was then striding out of the sunroom, through the various rooms of the house, and finally moving with her up the stairs. He pulled her into his room, shut and locked the door behind him, and stared at her. Ruby didn't miss how he kept clenching and unclenching his hands at his sides. But over the last two weeks she had come to read him very well. He was barely holding on to his control right now, and that was a very, very frightening realization.

"I think I need to show you that you are worthy, and that acting out like this over frivolous things means punishment." He grabbed the hem of his sweater and started to pull it off. He wore a stark white T-shirt underneath, but the thin material did nothing to hide the raw power that he exuded. He continued to stare at her as he undid his belt and pulled it from the loops of his slacks. She expected him to toss it aside, but instead he wrapped the leather around his hand. "Strip, Ruby." Voice low, but holding so much control, Gavin lowered his head slightly and stared at her, demanding she obey him with that look alone.

"What if I said no?" God, she was playing with fire, but she wanted to get burned, wanted to feel the flames lick over her skin until that was all she could feel. All she could think about was her mother's shitty little trailer, about how Gavin had looked into all of that, and knew how crummy her life was. All the pain, anger, embarrassment, and affection she felt was too much inside of her and all she wanted was to feel something else.

The corner of his mouth slowly lifted, but it wasn't a smile of amusement. It was one of sadistic satisfaction. Did he know *he* was playing into *her* hands, that she was trying to be the one in control right now, even if for one moment? He took a step forward.

She lifted her hands and touched the first button of her blouse. He stopped his advance and watched her continue. Her shirt was silky and smooth under her fingers. Popping the first button free of the hole, she continued up and did the same with each tiny mother of pearl button until the blouse hung open. Underneath she didn't wear a bra, but she did have a lacy camisole on. Slipping the shirt from her shoulder, she pulled the camisole up and over her head and it joined the shirt on the floor. The skirt she wore was tight, long and formfitting, and she reached behind to unzip it. Fear was still a heady emotion inside of her, and she wasn't foolish enough to think that she shouldn't be afraid of Gavin just because she felt more in control at the moment. When she was out of the skirt and only in a pair of stilettos that Gavin had especially picked out, she waited for his next move.

He came closer, walked around her, and she swore she could feel his hands on her when he wasn't even touching her. His presence was so intense that she couldn't help but hold her breath. Hands shaking from the turbulent emotions inside of her, she opened her eyes and stared up at him. Even in her heels he was so much taller than she was, and his broad shoulders blocked out the room behind him. They were all alone, but even if they had been in a roomful of people, she knew she would have felt as if it were just the two of them.

"You know, darling," he took a step closer and her nipples budded from the heat that came from his body. "I find it quite amusing that you think you are in control of this situation." Ruby didn't move, because there had been a part of her that knew nothing got by Gavin; she had been stupid to think that she had any kind of control over what was about to happen. "And the fact that your anger stems from your embarrassment that I looked into your life angers me to the point that I am blinded by it." She swallowed at his harsh voice. "No one's life is perfect or glamorous, even with all the money in the world." She looked down at the belt that was still wrapped around his hand and wondered if he would whip her embarrassment and all the other turbulent emotions out of her. He looked down, and when he lifted his head there was a sadistic smile tugging at his lips. "I know you're wondering how far I am going to go."

He took a step back and reached behind him to grab his shirt and pull it up over his head. His dark hair became slightly disheveled from the act. Right now he looked almost unhinged as he stared at her. She watched the hard, huge muscles of his chest flex. He was still in those loose slacks, but for some reason that made him seem even more dangerous than ever before. The air around him was heated, and there was a glint of excitement in his eyes.

"Yes." She answered him, but her voice cracked on the last letter from her fear, arousal, and deep-rooted need to see exactly how far he would go.

Ruby knew she should be scared to death, fear for her life even. But the part of her that she'd always thought sick and deranged wanted everything Gavin could give her. It had taken her time with her beautiful captor to make Ruby realize that she wasn't sick at all. There was nothing wrong with her needs even if they weren't ones that were considered "normal." She wasn't alone in this, and as she looked at Gavin, she knew that she had found the missing puzzle piece of her life. The strange thing was she hadn't even realized it had been missing until she had been thrust into this situation.

"You wanted this, Ruby, and I'm about to give you far more than you think you can handle."

Chapter Eleven

For several long seconds, all Gavin did was stare at Ruby as she stood before him naked and looking so fucking beautiful that he was starving for her. He kept tightening his hold on the belt wrapped firmly around his hand, and the images of bringing the smooth leather down across her ass and the back of her thighs had his cock hard and throbbing. "Turn around and press your chest to the wall beside you." His room was set up for the things he liked to do sexually, and he was about to experience Nirvana with his woman. Even from a distance, he saw the way her pulse beat wildly at the base of her throat, and he wanted to kiss and lick at her flesh, and feel the beat of that fear and anticipation under his tongue.

He tilted his chin in the direction he wanted her to go and stayed where he was as he watched her turn and make her way toward the wall. Her ass was lush even for her small frame, but the firm, high globes moved seductively as she walked to the wall. She looked so good pressed against the ice blue and black damask wallpaper. When he saw the side of her breast press against the wall, he moved closer to her. He bent and removed her shoes, and although he loved the way she looked in them with nothing else on, he didn't want her to have the extra height for this little fun they were going to have. Above her was a pulley system. The cord that adjusted the height was hidden beneath the headboard of the bed, and he walked over to it and grabbed it. Moving it so that the leather was lowered, he heard her quick gasp as she glanced up and saw what he was doing.

"What is that?" The shaky quality of her voice turned him on even more because it was that hesitance and lack of knowledge that had the monster deep inside of him coming forth with a vengeance.

"It's for you, my pet." He took her hands and lifted them up so he could attach the leather around them. He took a step to the side, adjusted the height, so she was forced to raise up on her toes to keep her balance, and then secured it so that she stayed in that position. Gavin moved several steps back until he had an unobstructed view of the glorious scene in front of him. Because she was on her toes, her entire body was stretched long, and all he could think about was running his tongue along every inch of her. She looked over her shoulder and he snapped his eyes to hers. "Turn the fuck back around. You do not move or speak without me specifically telling you to do just that." Her eyes widened, but she turned around and rested her forehead on the wall.

"Am I supposed to call you something? Master, Sir, something like that?" He let the belt unravel from his hand and took a step toward her. Without responding to her question, he pulled his arm back and brought the strip of leather forward. The sound of it hitting her flesh, and then of her gasp of pain, had him closing his eyes and groaning in pleasure. The red line instantly popped out along her creamy flesh, and his cock jerked forward at the sight. He brought the leather down across her ass once more, and she cried out, her head tilting back. He moved to the side so he could see her face and saw her eyes close and a tear slide down her cheek.

"The first one was because you spoke when I specifically told you not to." He gave her a moment to breathe through the pain, but he also knew she was aroused, saw the way she clenched her thighs together, and he was anxious to give her more. "And the second one was just because I loved the way your skin became red when the leather connected with your body." He moved closer to her and smoothed his hand across the two lines along her ass.

Her flesh was hot and slightly raised where the belt had struck, but as much as he knew that it had probably hurt like a bitch, he could practically smell the arousal coming from her.

He got on his haunches, grabbed her cheeks, and pulled them apart. He still had the belt in his hand, but he wanted her to feel it pressed against her leg, wanted her to realize that he wasn't nearly done with her yet. "Open your legs wide, Ruby. I want to see the pussy that belongs to me." She complied instantly, and he curled his fingers into the flesh of her ass. "Good girl, Princess." The scent of her arousal slammed into him. He stared at the sight of her slit, glistening with her cream. Her pussy hole was slightly open from the way he was holding her, and he didn't deny himself tasting her. Gavin leaned down and ran his tongue down her cleft, pressing the muscle to the tiny opening. Over and over he swirled it around her hole, licking and swallowing her juices, and needing more. Groaning against her slickened flesh, he pulled away, forcing himself to back off or he wouldn't be able to stop, and Gavin wasn't about to end their fun right now.

Moving back once again, he liked how she kept her legs open, loved the fact that her back was arched as she popped her ass out, as if seeking more. He would give her more, so much more until she was blind from her lust. "Tell me, darling, did you like the feel of my belt along your flesh?" Her eyes were still closed, her lips parted, and she seemed almost drugged. Good because he wanted her to enjoy this as much as he was.

"Yes." A strangled moan left her when he brought the belt across the back of her legs this time.

"To answer your earlier question, no, I do not want you to call me anything but Gavin." He brought the belt across her thighs again, and then her ass. Then Gavin found himself staring at her, almost in a trance as her flesh turned a vibrant red. "Tell me, Ruby, how good this makes you feel." Sweat beaded his brow as he continued to spank her repeatedly until she was crying harder than he had ever seen her do so before.

"It hurts so good." He tossed the belt aside and stared at the work he had done. Her entire ass and the back of her thighs were red, and he even saw some bruises starting to form. He was on his knees behind her a second later, smoothing his hands up and down her hot flesh, and then leaned in to run his tongue along her flesh. Gavin had his hands on either side of her legs as he licked, nipped, and kissed her raised and scorching skin. The scent of her arousal was even more potent the longer he went, and he saw the wetness coating her inner thighs. Dipping his head and licking at her cream, he groaned and murmured incoherent things. He was fervid for her, so aroused his dick was about to burst through his slacks, and all he could think about was the way the belt had sounded as it hit her flesh, and the noise she made after each hit.

"I'm going to fuck your ass tonight, darling." He ran his tongue along her pussy, sucked her clit into his mouth until she was grinding her cunt on his face, and then flattened his tongue and slid it up to the tight hole between the firm mounds of her bottom. Gavin had claimed every part of her so far, all except her ass, but that was going to be rectified tonight. Before he was unable to stop himself from just taking her right against this wall, he stood and lowered the pulley. Ruby sagged against his arms once he had her unrestrained. Gavin held her for several seconds, smoothing his hands up and down her back until her shaking subsided. "Do you want me to take every part of you, Princess?" She nodded. He gripped her nape gently but firmly and pulled her head back so she could look up at him. "Answer me when I ask you a question."

"Yes, Gavin, I want to be yours. I want you to own every part of me." As he stared into her sweet, delicate face, saw the way her pupils dilated from the truth of her words, he knew he would never be able to let this girl go. She was his, only his, and anyone that tried to take her away from him would know firsthand the wrath that could be had by his hand.

He could tell she was unsteady on her feet and knew that the endorphins were moving through her body at a fast pace. Picking her up and holding her close to his body, he kissed the top of her head. He was still high on the fact he needed to take her even higher, but he didn't want to push her to the point that he never got her back, and that was a very real possibility if he didn't control himself. Already he had been close to the edge, and it seemed that need grew faster inside of him every time he touched her.

Laying her on the bed, he took a moment to look at her. Gavin didn't miss the wince that covered her face at the sensitivity of her ass and thighs coming in contact with the bed, but that had him growing even more aroused. "Get on your belly and let me see what I am going to be fucking." Having her obey him immediately was arousing all in its own, but she didn't do that, and instead hesitated, looking up at him. And her reluctance was even more satisfying.

But he knew the game she was playing, knew that she wanted this pain to numb whatever she was feeling. He might not know exactly what it was, but he would find out. It could be because he hadn't told her he had looked into her background, but that seemed petty in the grand scheme of things. He had purchased her, spanked her until she came for him, and if she thought that he should divulge every little piece of information to her, then she would need to realize that her place in his life did not include that. He had feelings for her; she was his property, but she was also so much more to him. They were connected, and because of that they were one and the same.

"If you don't get on your belly and show me your ass, I will be forced to punish you again. And Ruby, it will not be a punishment you enjoy." That had her licking her lips and flipping onto her belly. Her ass was a glorious shade of red, with hints of purple and blue mixed in. Gavin reached out and smoothed a hand along the curve of her spine, over her rear, and down her thighs. She twitched, most likely from the discomfort, but she spread her legs slightly and he could see she was soaking wet for him. But her pussy wouldn't be his tonight. When she came he would be buried balls deep in her tight little ass.

Moving over to the dresser, he opened the top drawer and got out a string of pearls and a bottle of lube. Like the good girl he knew she could be, her eyes were closed, and she was in the same position he had left her. Making his way into the bathroom, he washed his hands and the pearls thoroughly and headed back into the room. For just a moment, he watched her back rise and fall as she breathed. She was nervous and anxious, that much he could pick up on instantly, and actually seeing what was going on with her and how he was making her feel had Gavin reaching down and placing a hand on his erection. Christ, he was so hard, hard enough that fluid leaked from the tip of his cock. He glanced down at the pearls he held, now warmed from the water and his touch. He had imagined doing this to her since the moment he had seen her, and although restraining her with the pearls was a visual orgasm all in its own, what he was about to do would be even more euphoric.

Placing a knee on the bed, he pulled her legs apart. "Lift your bottom, Ruby." She did so instantly and he gave one of her ass cheeks a swat. "So obedient." Her cunt was red and swollen from her desire, and so fucking wet. As much as he wanted to eat her out again, make her come with his tongue alone, he wasn't going to. Taking the strand of pearls and running them along the back of one of her legs, he watched her mouth open and heard her suck in a breath. He placed the necklace at the opening of her pussy, and inch by slow inch, he started to push the thick beads inside. She opened her eyes and made a small noise. He could see the way her pussy clamped down on the string of pearls, and his dick nearly tore through his pants at the sight. When all of it was inside of her except three beads, he reached for the lube, spread her cheeks apart, and just stared at the tight ring of muscle for a second. Tilting the bottle, he let the clear liquid slide down the crease of her ass and cover her hole. He used his thumb to spread it around and then pushed it inside, making sure she was nice and slick for when he shoved his dick into her.

"Oh." The one word came from her as he removed his thumb and replaced it with a finger and then added another one. Scissoring the digits inside of her, stretching her to be able to take his thick dick had sweat dripping down his spine. He needed this, needed her surrender like he needed to breathe. He had to step away and catch his breath, because seeing her pussy filled with the pearls, still able to feel the inner muscles of her ass clench and release around his fingers, had Gavin on the verge of coming as it was.

Removing his pants and stepping from them, he reached for the lube once more and coated his erection with it. Then he was right back behind her, guiding his dick into her ass. Hand on her neck and pressing her face into the mattress, he needed to make her know he was in charge, and needed to feel her complete surrender. The tip of his dick popped through the tight ring of muscle, and he let go of the root of his cock and started to push into her. He was mindful that she had never taken a man back here before, but that didn't mean he would go easy. He used his other hand and grabbed hold of her wrist, yanked her arm behind her, and pinned her wrist at the small of her back. Her other hand was by her face, the sheets bunched in her fist. The sensation of pushing through all of her hot, lube-slicked tightness had his head falling back and his eyes closing. Then he started moving back and forth, and the feeling of those beads wedged in her tight pussy, with only a thin layer of flesh separating him from them, had his balls drawing up tight. She tried to turn her head, but he pushed her face down on the bed and curled his fingers into her wrist harder. She mewled from the pleasure, but also pain, no doubt.

The air left him harshly when she squeezed her inner muscles. "If you fucking do that again this will be over before it even begins." He pulled almost out of her ass before thrusting back inside her hard enough that her upper body shifted forward on the bed. "It's good, Ruby. Christ, you are so fucking good." In and out he moved within her, increasing his speed every second until his entire body was covered in sweat and a few beads from his temple dripped onto her back to mix with her own perspiration. His hair was damp and the short strands stuck to his forehead. Looking down at where his dick was deep within her ass, he watched in voyeuristic pleasure as her pink flesh was stretched wide around him. "Is it good for you, darling?" He curled his fingers into her neck and she moaned. "Is the pain enough? Do you need more from me?"

"It's good." He let his gaze travel over the light bruises on her ass and let go of her wrist to smooth his hand over them. She kept her hand behind her back, and he was immensely pleased that he didn't have to tell her to do that. He was very close to coming, but he wanted to feel her clench around him as she found her own release. He slowed his pace and slipped his arm around her waist, lifting her up.

"Hold your weight up on your hands and knees." She did as he asked, and he moved his hand lower, took hold of the strand of pearls and then started pumping in and out of her. "You're going to come when I do, Princess." He was panting now, doing everything in his power not to come before she did. "Do you understand me, Ruby?" She nodded her head, but then breathed out her affirmation. Pulling out and resting the tip of his dick at her entrance, he slammed into her with so much force she nearly lost her balance. He did this repeatedly, and right when he felt the first ripple move along his shaft he slowly started to remove the strand from her pussy. She tossed her head back and cried out long and hard, and he pumped into her faster and harder while continuing to pull the pearls from her sweet body.

Her orgasm was like saccharine coating the air, and he inhaled it deeply and let his own orgasm burst forth like a fierce animal taking control. Groaning out and coming forcefully in her ass, he filled her up, marking her, fully claiming every fucking part of her until there would never be any doubt that she was his. When his pleasure subsided and he could see her arms shaking as she tried to stay upright, Gavin pulled out and collapsed on the bed beside her. She fell forward, breathing heavily, covered in perspiration, a beautiful flush covering her body. After a few minutes, she rolled onto her back and Gavin admired the way her large, taut breasts swayed from the action. She even had that light flush along her chest and belly. Her eyes were closed, but when he reached out and pushed a strand of her damp hair away, she opened her eyes and looked at him. Gavin didn't say anything for a moment, and just enjoyed looking at her with a post-euphoric glow surrounding her.

"That was intense."

Gavin continued to move the tips of his fingers along her forehead and down her cheek. He didn't say anything, but he felt the same way. She was perfect for him, the perfect masochist to his starving sadist. But as he looked at her, thought about all the things he had found out about her life, and thought about what Adelbert had said, he couldn't deny that having her here of her own free will would be even more pleasurable. He needed her to choose him, needed her to decide what she actually wanted, and not be surrounded by him or his things to do that. He thought about Adelbert's words, and how if she wasn't here of her own free will then that needed to be rectified. He didn't want to give her a choice, if he were being honest, but he knew that in order for their bond to form completely, so nothing could come between them, then Ruby needed to decide on her own.

You realize that this young woman could ruin you with nothing more than her walking away, and that scares the shit out of you.

There had never been anything that frightened Gavin except loneliness. But he could handle being alone. What he couldn't handle was not being with Ruby.

"Is everything okay?" She turned onto her side, but he moved onto his back. The air chilled as her emotions shifted.

"Everything is fine, Princess." But it wasn't, and Gavin didn't like that feeling.

Chapter Twelve

Ruby had been on edge all day, and she didn't know why. Well, that wasn't necessarily true. She knew why she was on edge and felt so uncertain. Ever since Gavin had taken her ass, a couple of days ago, he had seemed to distance himself from her. He still slept beside her, still held her, but she felt his detachment. Had she done something wrong, had he realized she wasn't what he wanted? All these questions slammed into her head, over and over again.

Ruby couldn't explain the hollowness that she felt, and often found herself staying in her room and looking out the windows, watching Drika tend to the grounds. This sudden change in him just didn't make sense, especially with what he had said to her, and all the things they had done together.

Turning away from the window, she moved over to the bed and sat down. Maybe Gavin had found another woman that he enjoyed more than her. Maybe he really was as bad as she originally thought and wanted a harem of women. Maybe he had just been breaking her in, making her trust him, want him, and then he'd turn his back and show her that she truly was nothing. But no, even after thinking that, she knew it wasn't the truth. She tried to rationalize that he was busy with work, and maybe that was why he was giving her this cold shoulder. Talking to him had gotten her nowhere. He dismissed her questions as if they meant nothing, but she had glimpsed something shift behind his eyes. Emotion maybe? Either way, she was starting to feel like an outsider, which hurt a lot since she had finally come to terms with the fact that she wanted Gavin.

There was a knock on her door and she stood and clasped her hands behind her back. The door opened and Gavin stood on the other side, wearing a black pinstripe suit. The white shirt and blood red silk tie stood out, making him look powerfully controlled. His cufflinks flashed as the sunlight hit them.

"How have you been, Ruby?" He stared at her stoically. He was the master of keeping his composure and not showing his emotions, and right now he had a wall in front of him. Ruby couldn't very well say they knew everything about each other. God, she hated not knowing why he was acting like this, and had gone cold on her.

"Have I done something wrong?" she asked for what seemed like the hundredth time, not bothering to answer his question. Her clear disobedience should have earned her some kind of delicious punishment, but this isolation from his attention was painful.

"Why would you think that?" He didn't move from the doorway. Her anger mounted at the lack of emotion he showed. So she acted out.

"Because you've done nothing but ignore me for the last few days. Ever since you fucked me in the ass." She felt her face heat from her crass words. She had always been more reserved, even living with a mother that was anything but. But she didn't fear punishment from Gavin, didn't even want it right now. At this moment she was angry and hurt and felt like she had been discarded.

"You're acting like a child again, Ruby." Her hands shook from her emotions, and she pressed them flat on her outer thighs.

"Maybe I am, but I don't give a fuck." She would not cry, not show an expression, although she had already failed at the latter. "How can you do that to a person?" He lifted a dark eyebrow. "How can you take someone, make them want you, care for you, and then just push them aside without any reason or explanation?"

"I always have a reason for what I do." That pissed her off even more, and she moved closer until they stood toe to toe.

"You bought me, brought me to this place, and away from my life—"

"You didn't have a life before I came around, Ruby. You were just surviving."

The tears she had tried to stop fell now, and she brushed them away. "You're a bastard." She said those three words on a whisper. She expected him to grab her, turn her around and spank her ass until she couldn't sit. That pain would have been welcome. But what he said in response surprised her.

"Yes, I am, Ruby, but I never claimed to be anything else." He took a step toward her, but she held her ground and looked him right in his cold blue eyes.

"How do you see yourself?"

"W-What do you mean?"

"How do you see yourself in my life? Do you think we are a couple, that you're my girlfriend?" He moved a step closer, and she took one back. "Do you think I will take you on dates, introduce you to people I know?" He took another step, and she kept retreating. "Do you see yourself as my wife?" Her tears were falling faster, and her vision was blurred. "Answer me." He yelled out those words, and she flinched from the anger in them.

"I guess I didn't know what I thought." That was a lie. She hadn't thought they would get married or anything like that, because what she felt for him went deeper than a certificate could declare, even after only a few weeks. But maybe he thought she had seen them as going out or something. She was so much younger than he was, and clearly she had just been his little pussy to play with as he pleased. God, it hurt to think that way.

He moved away from her and nodded slowly. "Well, we need to rectify that then." What the hell did that mean? He reached out and grabbed her arm, tugging her forward and out the door. She had to all but run just to keep up with his quick, long strides, and soon she found herself down the stairs, out the front door, and shoved into the back seat of the limo. Ruby righted herself just as Gavin sat down and closed the door behind him. The limo pulled forward, and she pushed her hair out of her face and looked at him.

"What are you doing?" He didn't answer, he wouldn't even look at her. Minutes later they were pulling onto the airstrip, and he was hauling her out the door. "Gavin, what are you doing?" She dragged her feet, but he was stronger than she was and easily pulled her along. Then they were on the jet, and she was pushed onto one of the leather seats. She was still crying because all she could think about was that he was taking her back to those human trafficking guys. "Why are you doing this? What did I do?" He finally looked at her, and she saw a flicker of emotion pass over his face.

"You didn't do anything. I'm taking you back to your old life, Ruby, since the only reason you are here is because you were taken from that." The doors closed, and it was a few minutes before the plane started to taxi.

"You don't want me anymore?" God, he wanted to take her back to that shitty world. She had nothing, nowhere to go. There was a time not long ago at all that she would have longed for this day, but now she hated it.

Ruby had fallen asleep a couple of hours ago, but they were due to land soon. Gavin leaned back, with only the one overhead light on in the main cabin. He watched her, saw the way her chest rose and fell under the light pink floral shirt she wore. He had been hard on her, had been very cold toward her for the last few days, but he had been doing a lot of thinking. After he had taken her, had used the pearls on her, all he could think about was the fear of her leaving. The words that Adelbert had spoken to him had been cemented in his mind. He wanted her, fuck he wanted her with his last breath, but he had a terrible fear of losing her. The only way he knew to ensure that she stayed with him, that their bond was solidified, was to take her back to her old life and have her decide if she wanted him or her freedom.

Maybe it wasn't the best-laid plan, because in reality she could leave if she wanted to even if she chose him, but at least he would know that she was with him of her own free will. The plane descended and landed, and after twenty minutes they were allowed to exit. "Ruby, darling, wake up." Over the past few days he had kept his distance. He hadn't shown her affection, but it hadn't been a punishment, just a way for him to get his thoughts in order.

She roused herself, rubbed the sleep from her eyes, and then after a few seconds, realized where she was. She sat up straighter and he looked into her face. He hated that she looked so forlorn. "We're here?"

He nodded. Her mother's trailer was a twenty-minute ride from the airstrip.

Once off the plane and in the limo, he took note that she stayed to herself, wouldn't look at him, and said nothing. "I have something for you." When she looked at him, he reached for the small, dark duffel beside him. He handed it to her, and she seemed reluctant to take it. "I am not leaving you without anything. Inside there is money to help you until you're on your feet, legal documents, and clothing."

"Why are you doing this?" She took the bag, but there was so much pain in her voice it broke his heart.

"I'm not doing this to hurt you, Princess." She shook her head and looked out the window.

"Yes, you are. You thrive on the pain of others."

He didn't respond for a minute because it was true to an extent.

"I just want you to know that you have a choice. That I am giving you a choice."

When she looked at him there was anger in her face. "If that was what this was about why make this big production? Why ignore me, make me feel unwanted, like I did something wrong?"

"Because I needed to think and needed you to realize that you do have a choice in how your life plays out. I don't want to let you go, don't want to know that you might leave me because you never had the option to go back to your life. That was the fear I was holding on to."

She stared at him, not saying anything, but he saw in her face she understood what he was saying.

They rode in silence the rest of the way, but he didn't press her for conversation or her thoughts. He had said what he needed to, and it was up to her to make her choice. When the limo pulled to a stop in front of her mother's shitty trailer, Ruby opened the door and began to climb out. It was very late, but lights shined through windows that looked like newspaper stood in for curtains. The neighborhood was rundown, falling apart, and debilitated.

Gavin reached out right before Ruby excited and grabbed her wrist. She stopped and looked over at him.

"I am not discarding you." He had to make her see that, and he'd say it over and over again. They held each other's gaze. "I just want you to know that you have a choice. You are not my captive, no matter how much I liked the idea. Maybe I shouldn't have treated you as anything but the treasure you are to me, but I did what I had to do to make you realize that you have options, and for me to understand that you needed to pick what you want in life." And he would keep telling her that until it was so solid inside of her that she never doubted it. The anger slowly drained from her face. "And I do care for you, Princess. So very much." Her breath hitched, but she said nothing, just nodded.

He hadn't meant to go soft right before she walked away because he knew it went against the grain of who he was and how he had tried to distance himself from her. He never claimed to be a good man, or a noble one. He was who he was and didn't apologize for it. But seeing her walk away had anger and pain the likes of which he had never felt before moving through him at an astounding rate. She pulled her hand away, climbed from the back of the limo, and shut the door behind her. All Gavin could do was watch her walk away and hope she ended up choosing him even though she hadn't been given a choice in the beginning.

Ruby stared at her mom's trailer. It might have only been a few weeks that she had been gone, but the life she had led with Gavin made this place look even worse. She felt Gavin watching her even though the doors were closed, and the windows tinted. She took a step forward, not sure if she actually planned to go in there or if she was just forcing herself to move away from the limo and the life it promised. She hated that he'd thought he needed to distance himself to make his point before helping her understand what he was trying to do.

She began to realize that she *was* thankful to be given a choice. Of course, she was still angry, and hated the way things had transpired, but if she was going to have any kind of life, she couldn't rely on anyone but herself.

A man stumbled out of the front door of her mother's trailer, a bottle of liquor in hand. He scratched his protruding belly and belched loud enough that she heard it over the music. It wasn't one of the men she had seen her mother with when Ruby lived there, so this must be a new piece of shit boyfriend. The guy leaned against the warped and rotted banister of the porch and chugged half of the alcohol from the bottle. She heard her mom yell something, but Ruby had already taken a step back. This had never been her home.

Turning, she saw that Gavin was now out of the limo and standing beside the open door. His face showed nothing, but his eyes held deep affection, and she could have sworn fear. "This isn't the life I want. It isn't the life I *ever* wanted." She had known that when she first left, but seeing it again made it that much more permanent.

"Tell me what you want, Princess." Gavin had always been so strong, but right now he sounded almost... fragile. Ruby looked at the fat slob still leaning against the railing, looked around at the rundown and already half-dead neighborhood, and knew that she had never belonged here. Looking back at Gavin, she didn't see his money or his expensive suits. She didn't think about the life she had with him across the ocean or his big estate. All she thought about was that *he* was the only one who had made her feel like she was worthy, and that what she wanted wasn't wrong. He accepted her, and embraced what she wanted, because that was what he wanted, too. Their lives may not have started in the best of ways, but she had to believe everything happened for a reason. He was the man that she had grown to care for and to trust. She didn't want the bag of money that she held, or to be anywhere else if Gavin wasn't there.

"I want *you*." She moved toward him and he immediately embraced her.

"I just wanted you to come to me of your own free will, darling." Ruby closed her eyes and just absorbed the feeling of being in his arms. "Let's go home."

As long as she was with Gavin, she was home.

Epilogue

Gavin sat in the corner, the shadows concealing him, and the moonlight moving through the open window. The summer breeze ruffled the lace curtains, moved along the edge of the duvet over Ruby, and then touched the tips of her hair. He had been away on business for the last week, and even though it was the middle of the night, he had come home as soon as soon as he had finished with work.

The last three years had been filled with a lot of turbulent emotions: happiness, pain and heartache, healing and love, and then finally hope. Ruby was his, would always be his, and even if they didn't need a legal document to prove that, Gavin had asked Ruby to marry him. They had wed a month later on the property, and seeing her draped in strands of pearls, that little lacy cream off-the-shoulder dress, and her dark hair falling over her shoulders, had made Gavin realize that this woman could destroy him.

He had bought her from a human auction block, knew that she had been taken from her home, and sold to the highest bidder. He should feel shame that he had been the one to purchase her even all these years later, but the truth was that he'd never felt that emotion. And then after he had taken her back to the run-down trailer park that she'd lived in with her mother, when Ruby had thrown herself back into his arms, he had known he would never let her go.

He had gotten his vasectomy reversed because he knew one day he wanted a family with the woman that he had grown to love. And then a year after they had been together, locked away in his European home and enjoying each other in dark, delicious pleasure-filled ways, she had become pregnant. Although he had been prepared for this, and Ruby had known that one day they would share the joy of creating a family together, her pregnancy had still been a shock to both of them. Before Ruby, Gavin had never wanted a family, never wanted a woman to keep as more than a sexual plaything. Ruby had been frightened, but deep down he had seen the anticipation of her holding a child, and of being a better mother than her own had been. There had been happiness, and Gavin realized that this young woman had made him see that without her in his life, he was nothing. He was a shell of a man, a hollow, empty soul.

And then she had lost the baby three months into the pregnancy. It hadn't been because his appetite for sadistic pleasure had been too much because the moment he had found out she carried his baby, he had put his selfish desires aside. There had been nothing but sweetness and gentle touches from him, and it had been enough as long as his child and the woman he loved were okay. His dark desires hadn't gone away, they never would, but he had suppressed them.

She had been with pain and heartache.

For months, she had been in this cave of despair, consumed by her grief, and there had been nothing he could do that had helped ease her pain. He had been tortured with her, and it had been like a searing hot knife slicing right through his heart. Every time he had looked at her, and saw her tears or this far-away expression, that pain had intensified inside of him. Taking her into town to go shopping, or suggesting they go away to a private island and not think about anything, hadn't gotten more than a shake of her head and her sadness intensifying.

But as the months had passed, she had started to heal, and he gave her more love than any person could possibly handle. He had taken time off work, just spending it with her, telling her that she was the only thing in his life that was worth anything. He hadn't been in a hurry to have another baby, especially if they had to experience that pain again, but he wanted her to know that he was there for her.

He brought himself back to the present when he heard the soft sound that had Ruby slowly rising. The sheet fell around her waist, and he was pleased to see she was nude and had her pearl choker on. Since he had brought her back to the mansion three years ago he had told her that he wanted her nude while sleeping, and that she was to wear the pearls at all times. It was his visual brand of ownership, but elegant enough that it accented her innocence and beauty.

He glanced down at the large swells of her breasts and felt his shaft start to thicken. He was still seated in the shadows, and although it was voyeuristic, he grew even harder. Gavin watched as she stood, her body fuller now, and her hair long enough that when she had it in a braid and over her shoulder it fell past her breast. She grabbed her robe and slipped it on and walked right by him without realizing he could have reached out and run his finger along her thigh.

When she was out of the room, he slowly stood, removed his suit jacket and tie, tossed it over the chair, and went for his cufflinks. He headed to the room directly across from theirs. He leaned against the doorframe and watched as his wife fed their four-month-old daughter. Willasandra, or Willa as they often called her, had a thatch of dark hair and blue eyes that reminded him of the summer sky. Willa reached up and started playing with the end of Ruby's braid, and his wife started humming a soft lullaby. He could stand there forever and just watch them.

They hadn't been trying to get pregnant, and when Ruby had, he'd seen the fear on her face. With each passing month that fear had become a little less, and then there had been hope. When his baby girl had been born, and he had looked in her eyes for the very first time, this hardness that had always been a part of him had cracked fully away. He had the two loves of his life. The sadistic bastard that he had associated himself with for far too long realized these two females were the most important thing to him.

For long minutes, all he did was watch Ruby with Willa. He could see his daughter's eyelids start to droop, and then she fell asleep. Ruby fixed her robe over her breasts, stood, and laid the baby down in the crib. For a few seconds, he just stared at her, and then he turned and gave them some privacy. Gavin went back into the bedroom, removed his clothing, and headed into the bathroom to clean up. He ached for Ruby, wanted her soft skin rubbing along his, wanted her breathy moans filling his ears, and craved the sweet flavor of her on his tongue. He desired to see her body flushed red from his spankings and wanted the indentations of the pearls he used on her to cover her form.

He took a shower, and once out and dried, he stepped back into the room. The lights were still off, but he saw Ruby sitting on the edge of the bed. She was nude once more, the light from the bathroom and the light of the moon bathing her body. His cock hardened instantly.

"I missed you," she said softly.

"I missed you, too, baby," he said, just as low, and turned off the bathroom light. He took a step toward her, looked at her full breasts, let his gaze slide down to her slightly rounded belly, and stopped at the bare mound of her pussy. She kept her sweet little cunt nice and bare for him, sweet and soft. She was his, and every part of her body belonged to him. Gavin could use her any way he saw fit, pleasure her until she screamed out for him to give her more. And he would do this because it was what *Ruby* wanted.

"I didn't know you were coming back tonight," she said on a breath, and he could tell she was getting aroused. Her breathing was changing slightly, her breasts rising and falling as she stared at him.

"How much did you miss me, Ruby?" he said on a low, deep voice, and felt his own desire rising higher.

"You know how much." She stood, and then immediately got onto the bed. Now on her knees, her legs spread slightly, and the view of her pussy on clear display, he groaned low in his throat. "Every part of me aches for your touch and hands, for your breath and cock... I just want you, Gavin."

She made him feel like his dick would explode if he wasn't buried inside of her tight, wet, and hot pussy. He moved closer to her and stopped when he reached the edge of the bed. He stared at her, took in every dip and hollow of her body. She had been tiny and thin when he had bought her from those human traffickers, but over the last three years, and since having Willa, her body was filled out. She was womanlier now, filled out in all the right places.

"Lay on your belly, baby." He watched as she listened to him immediately, and he gave an approving growl. He gave one of her ass cheeks a spank. "So obedient, Ruby." Gavin moved onto the bed, spread her legs as wide as they would go, and stared at her pussy. Her cunt was red and swollen, and already so fucking wet. The fact that her hair was still in a braid, and that he could see her neck and the beautiful choker wrapped around it, had his balls drawing up tight.

Gavin reached for the end table, opened the drawer, and pulled out the silk satchel that held the strands of pearls he used to pleasure her with. Taking the strand of pearls, he ran them along her back. She turned her head, closed her eyes, and parted her lips. Goose flesh popped along her arms and legs, and he bent his head and brought his tongue along the dip of her spine. Taking her hands and placing them at the small of her back, he used the reinforced pearls to secure her wrists. He then took the tether attached to it and hooked the clasp to the small hook on her choker. The length of the pearls now lay flush with her spine.

Picking up the middle one, he gave the strand a light tug until she lifted her bottom half off the bed and braced herself on her knees.

"Spread your legs wide, baby."

She opened her eyes and made a small noise. His dick hardened even more at the sight. She was so fucking wet. He slipped his fingers through her folds, coated his digits with her cream, and then lifted them to his mouth. Gavin couldn't help but suck them clean. She tasted heavenly, and after being away from her for a week, he felt starved for her in every way imaginable. And then he had his face buried between her thighs. He licked and sucked, swallowed her arousal, and growled for more. Spanking an ass cheek over and over again, he felt her flesh heat beneath his palm, and then started to do the same to the other cheek. The moans that came from her fueled his dark desire.

"Oh, Gavin." Those words came from her as he removed his mouth from her pussy and placed his finger at her entrance. He pumped that finger in and out of her and then added another one. Scissoring the digits, stretching her because he liked the feeling of his fingers in her sweet body, of making her accept his girth had sweat dripping down his chest. He needed this, needed her like he needed to breathe.

"There will never be anyone else for me, Ruby."

She gasped out after he spoke.

"You're mine. Tell me that you belong to me." He gently bit her right ass cheek, loved that she cried out in pain and pleasure, and did the same to the other cheek.

"I'm yours; you know this," she sighed. "I will always be yours."

Gavin couldn't control himself any longer. He straightened and removed his fingers from her body. After sucking them clean, he turned her head to the side, took her chin in a firm hold, and kissed her hard. He forced her to taste herself on his lips and tongue. When she was begging him for more, he straightened once more and guided his dick into her.

Hand now on her neck, he pressed her face into the mattress. Gavin needed to make her know he was in charge, that he was the one that had the control. He might own her body, but she owned every single fucking part of him. His dick slid right into her welcoming heat, and he let go of the root of his cock and grabbed her waist. He knew he would leave pretty bruises on her creamy white flesh, and he needed to see those marks.

The sensation of pushing into her, feeling her clench around his length, and of her moaning out his name, nearly had Gavin coming right then and there. He started moving back and forth, and his balls drew up tight from his release rising to the surface.

"I'm so close, Gavin," she panted out.

"Give it to me, baby."

She mewled from the pleasure, and when he dug his fingers into her body harder, she cried out from the pain. The air left him harshly when she squeezed her pussy muscles around him. He pulled almost out of her, but before he popped out, he thrust back inside her hard enough that her upper body shifted forward on the bed.

"It's so fucking good, Ruby. Goddammit, you feel so fucking good." In and out he moved within her, increasing his speed every second. Looking down at where his dick was deep within her pussy, he watched in voyeuristic pleasure as she was stretched wide around him. "Is it good for you, sweetheart?"

She moaned. "It's good. It's so good."

He was very close to coming, but he wanted to feel her clench around him as she found her own release first. He slowed his pace and slipped his arm around her waist, lifting her up. With his other hand he quickly undid the clasp at her neck, removed the pearls from her wrist so she was free, and pulled her back flush with his chest. He started pumping in and out of her faster.

"You're going to come, baby." He panted hard, doing everything in his power not to come before she did. "Do you understand me, Ruby?"

She nodded before she uttered a breathy yes. Pulling out and resting the tip of his dick at her entrance, he slammed into her with so much force she nearly fell forward. He felt the first ripple of her orgasm move along his shaft. She tossed her head back, rested it on his shoulder, and cried out long and hard. This was what he wanted, her sweet, sweet surrender. He inhaled deeply and let his own orgasm come forth like a fierce animal. Groaning out, he filled her up, marking her, fully claiming every fucking part of her. When his pleasure subsided, Gavin pulled out and collapsed on the bed beside her. She fell forward, breathing heavily and covered in sweat. He watched her, loved that she was gone in this moment, and then he brushed away a lock of hair that fell from her braid. After a few minutes, she rolled onto her back and Gavin pulled her close. He just held her and enjoyed that she was here with him.

Gavin moved the tips of his fingers along her forehead and down her cheek. She smiled, and the sigh that left her was one of contentment and of being thoroughly loved. When the sound of Willa crying pierced the silence, he kissed Ruby on the forehead and got off the bed.

"I can go to her," Ruby said sleepily.

"No, Princess, I'll get her." He grabbed a pair of lounge pants and moved out of room and into Willa's. She wailed in a tiny little voice, and he cooed at her when he got to the crib. His presence made her cry harder, and he picked up his little daughter and cradled her to his chest. He hummed softly and moved over to the chair. Once seated, he started rocking, and soon Willa fell back asleep. He didn't stop rocking, and when he glanced up, he saw Ruby standing in the doorway. He still had a darkness inside of him that only she could sate, but she his sweet masochist to and he was her wicked sadist.

She was the only one that could tame him.

"I love you," she said softly.

"I love you, too, darling."

She smiled and then turned away and went back into their room.

He was a better man now because of Ruby and Willa, and because of them, he'd fight every day to be the husband and father they deserved.

The End

Read an exclusive excerpt from **HIS,** a dark erotic romance by
Jenika Snow

His

USA TODAY BESTSELLING AUTHOR
JENIKA SNOW

WARNING: *This is not a traditional love story. This book does not end in the normal "happily ever after." There are no wedding bells at the end, no love being professed, or long walks on the beach. If that is the type of story you want this book probably isn't for you. This book is fiction and contains material that some readers may find offensive.*

Bethany Sterling comes from a privileged family, one that believes in modern-day marriage arrangements. On the outside she plays the part of the perfect daughter, but on the inside she is looking for another way out. She hides what she really wants in life, because showing her dreams and aspirations is a weakness she can't afford to reveal.

As soon as Abe saw her he knew that he would go to any lengths to make her his. He is trained to be lethal, stealthy, and have no remorse in his actions. His needs take control of him until he is nothing more than a machine intent on following his plan.

Bethany finally gets her wish for a new life, but it isn't how she envisioned it. Now with Abe she realizes that his need for her runs deep. She shouldn't want him, but she is also compelled and attracted to him.

It is those turbulent emotions pulling her in different directions that will have Bethany deciding how far she is willing to go.

"So, ask, Bethany."

The room grew still and quiet and she hated that he could look so unaffected. *Why are you surprised?* He wasn't the one chained up like a rabid dog, and in fact this little situation was probably his disgusting fantasy. "Why did you do it?" That seemed like the safest question to ask first.

"I told you. I saw you, wanted you, and so I took you."

God, he said it so icily that goose bumps rose on her arms. "You took me because you wanted me?" It was a straightforward answer, but it still didn't make any sense.

"Yes."

"But you're my father's head of security. He trusted you with his life."

The sound of him grinding his teeth was overly loud in the room. "He is still alive, isn't he? He was never harmed while in my protection, never so much as threatened." His voice went lower, deeper, and she knew this was a conversation that was steering away from what they should be talking about.

"What do you plan on doing with me?" She hated asking that question because she almost didn't want to know what he was going to say.

"This is what I plan on doing with you." He leaned back on the couch and didn't say anything after that for several seconds.

Bethany felt everything in her body grow cold and numb by his statement. "Your plan is to keep me locked away in this cabin?"

"Yes, that is exactly what I have planned." He leaned forward, bracing his forearms on his thighs. "That is my plan for the time being." He held her gaze with his own penetrating one. "Until I can trust you."

"And then what?" Her pulse beat frantically at the base of her throat, and it was becoming increasingly more difficult to breathe.

"And then we'll start our life together."

She shook her head, but it was more of an automatic response than her responding to his statement. "I don't want you. I don't want any of this." The last part was a gasp of air and words.

"You do." He didn't crack a smile, didn't show any emotion, for that matter.

Bethany didn't bother arguing that point, and instead decided on what she wanted to ask him next. "You said you wouldn't rape me." She stated it point-blank, and when she looked at him it was to see him nod once again. God, she wished she could read him, but he was as hard and cold as stone.

"I don't rape women."

"My family will come looking for me, and they'll find me." Bethany swallowed. She felt like she was just repeating herself, but when he would barely give her a straight answer she had nothing else to go on. "You know they have money, and they won't stop until I'm found." Sitting up straighter gave her the semblance of being stronger, but she felt weak inside. "Steven has money, and I'm set to wed in a few months." At her words, a very dark cloud seemed to settle over him, and the room suddenly felt much colder. She knew she should just stop.

"I'm going to tell you who and what I am, and that even if they did find you, I wouldn't let them have you."

Everything inside of Bethany was at a standstill. God-awful thoughts of what secrets he held filled her mind.

"I was born to nothing, and grew up with nothing. When I was found in a dirty back alley behind a known whorehouse and asked to channel my energy to something else, I took the opportunity." There was a sliver of emotion in his voice, but it was rage. "My mother was a whore herself, and my father the man that raped her. To say my mother loathed me and where I came from was an understatement. I was a burden to her, a reminder of the filthy life she lived, and the consequences of the path she had chosen." He leaned in close, and Bethany felt her eyes grow wider. "When I say I don't, and would never rape a woman, I mean just that, but that doesn't mean I won't urge you to open your eyes and see what is right in front of you."

Bethany didn't know what to say, because although she didn't want to sympathize with the man holding her prisoner, she also was human, and could only imagine the kind of life and anguish a child born into that life would have led.

"I was trained by some men that others would consider very bad, conditioned and sculpted to not let my emotions come into play, and to handle their business."

"And what business is that?"

He didn't respond right away, but stared at her with his cold, calculating gaze. "This world will eat you up, Bethany, without even caring." He reached out and brushed a stray piece of hair away. "I know what it is to feel like you were born to strangers, to live in a world that didn't want you. I fought every day of my life to survive, saw death, violence, drugs and abuse the likes I will never want you to see." He was opening up to her, showing her a side the past year had never revealed. This man had a lot of hidden things, been scarred in ways she would never even know. "Will I tell you I'm a good man?"

His eyes were so dark, so frigid and *real*. She loved and hated this attraction, but still found herself staring at him, looking at every curve and dip of his muscles, the way his short dark hair barely touched his forehead, and his square jaw that seemed so masculine. This man was so lethal in more than just the killing kind of way.

"No, I won't because I'm not a good man, Bethany. In fact, I am the furthest thing from a good man as they come."

"But I'm not yours. If you would have talked to me, maybe we could have started a relationship—"

He shook his head, stopping her from finishing her sentence. "Do I look like the traditional type of man that goes and asks women out on dates, smokes cigars and drinks scotch with their fathers?" He lifted a dark eyebrow, almost in a mocking manner. "I am a trained killer, Bethany, and I'll keep telling you that until you fully realize the man that you are sitting in front of right now has already claimed you as his."

She brushed a stray tear away, not knowing why she was crying. Her own emotions were wild and crazy. "No. I'll never be a man's that has to resort to this—"

And then he was on her before she could even grasp what in the hell he was doing. He used his upper body to press her back to the couch, and used the surprise of his attack to wedge his hips between her thighs. She parted her lips and screamed out, but he slapped a hand over her mouth. Bethany sucked in air through her nose, in and out, faster and faster until stars started to dance in front of her vision. "Calm down."

She blinked the stars away, knowing she needed to focus because passing out while he was on top of her and clearly aroused was a frightening thought.

"No one can hear you, Bethany, so screaming is pointless." He let those words sink in before continuing. "I'm going to remove my hand, and you're not going to scream, okay?" Although he did phrase it like a question, she knew it wasn't an option.

She nodded, and he slowly removed his hand. "If no one can hear me, than why stop me?" She was still breathing hard, but the need to pass out had subsided.

"Because I don't like the sound of it." He leaned in close and she held her breath, waiting to see what he would do. When their lips were only an inch apart she turned her head, but he must have anticipated the move because he gripped her chin and forced her head back so she was looking at him again. He ground his erection into her and she hated that her body started to warm. His dick was pressed right up against her pussy, and even with layers of clothing separating them she swore she could feel how big and long he was.

"Please, don't do this."

He ground harder into her, rotating his hips so he rubbed her clit, and hot tears spilled out of her eyes. "You like it, even though you're crying, Bethany."

She hated that he was right, wanted to destroy her traitorous body for becoming warm and wet, and so damn pliant under him. He pulled back just enough to look at her chest. With no bra on, her nipples stabbed through the thin material. She was humiliated, horrified, and started crying harder because her pussy grew wetter at the gentle yet persistent thrusting of his hips between her legs.

"I bet if I touched your cunt right now you'd be so damn wet for me." He slowly lifted his gaze from her breasts to her face again. And then like the bastard he was, he slipped his hand between her thighs and pressed the material right on her moist panties. He leaned in close to her ear, pushed a piece of her hair away, and said, "I knew you'd be wet." He started rubbing his hand in slow circles over her. "I knew you were waiting for someone to come and open you up, take you away from the world that you don't belong in." He applied just a little bit of pressure and she felt tendrils of an orgasm rising violently to the surface. "I know if I kept this up you'd come undone for me right now, wouldn't you?" He continued to rub her clit until she knew that if he didn't stop the orgasm that she didn't want to have—at least she told herself that over and over again—would steal her and somehow make this seem okay. Bethany didn't want to just roll over and surrender to him.

Now Available

A Beautiful Prison: Audio

Connect with Jenika

Who is Jenika Snow? She is the pseudonym of a mother, wife and nurse. She lives in the too hot northeast with her husband and their two daughters. She's been writing professionally since 2009, writes in many different sub-genres in Erotic Romance, and is a *USA Today* bestselling author.

Web: http://www.jenikasnow.com/
Email: Jenika_Snow@yahoo.com
FB: http://www.facebook.com/jenikasnow

Made in the USA
Charleston, SC
15 April 2016